Strong Silent SEAL
SEALs of Coronado

Paige Tyler

Cover Design by Gemini Judson, Cover Gems
Editing by Wizards in Publishing

ISBN-13: 978-1535331272

ISBN-10: 1535331275

Dedication

With special thanks to my extremely patient and understanding husband, without whose help and support I couldn't have pursued my dream job of becoming a writer. You're my sounding board, my idea man, my critique partner, and the absolute best research assistant any girl could ask for!

Thank you.

Wedding planner Felicia Bradford is in trouble. Mercenaries are holding her sister hostage and threatening to kill her unless Felicia helps them steal top secret information from the Navy's Special Operations Headquarters. Having no other way to access the base, she pulls a gun on the first man in a Navy uniform she finds, demanding he get her through the gate.

Navy SEAL Logan Dunn just got back from a mission in Syria and is looking for a little downtime to relax. That plan goes out the window when a beautiful woman shoves a gun in his back and begs him to do something she clearly doesn't want to do. Logan does what any Navy SEAL would do in the same situation—he saves the girl and takes out the bad guys.

But their actions that day kick off a crazy chain of events, including a fast-burning whirlwind romance, an out-of-control sister, an insane covert plot involving a defecting Russian pilot, a mercenary bent on revenge, and a sunrise wedding for a bride who never wakes up before noon.

Getting through her sister's kidnapping will look like a piece of cake compared to what comes next.

Prologue

Northern Syria

CAN YOU REMIND me who the good guys are again?" Nash Cantrell whispered to Logan as he scanned the ridgeline above the dark ravine where they hid.

Leading Petty Officer Logan Dunn peered through his night vision goggles at the ragtag collection of freedom fighters, covert government operatives, and men who were probably closer to being terrorists than allies with them in the ravine, and decided he could understand why his fellow SEAL had a hard time figuring out which people to keep in front of them and which ones they could trust to cover their six.

Logan and Nash, along with two other SEALs—Chasen Ward and Dalton Jennings—had been in Syria for over a month supporting the various fighters standing against President Assad's regime and ISIL. The Syrian civil war some people already referred to as World War III via proxy involved a bewildering array of combatants, including the Russian Special Forces known as Spetsnaz, and even though this was Logan's third tour over here in the last eight months, he had to admit it was damn near impossible to identify the players without a score card.

Bottom line, the situation over here was a cluster fuck, and a man intent on making it home alive would be smart not to trust any of these people.

Logan gave Nash a smile. "Easy—you, me, Chasen, and Dalton. Assume everyone else around is a bad guy and you won't be disappointed."

"I can work with that," Nash said. "But does it include the guys from SOG too?"

Logan glanced at the four men crouching twenty feet away from them in the very darkest—and farthest—corner of the ravine. Being part of the CIA's Special Operation Group tended to make those guys feel like they were in their own world, but, in this case, it seemed mostly by choice. Even though he and the other SEALs were supposedly on this mission to provide direct backup to the covert paramilitary operations officers from the CIA, the four men hadn't said a single word to them the entire time. Not during the mission brief, the flight out on the chopper, or since they'd touched down. Logan didn't even know most of the guys' names. He thought the leader of the group was Joe—maybe.

"We cover those guys because it's what we're here to do," Chasen answered Nash's question. "But don't put yourself in a position of having to depend on them to save your ass. You understand what I'm saying?"

Logan didn't have to ask for clarification, and neither did the other guys. SOG operatives came from the top United States Special Forces programs, including SEALs, so it's not like they were slouches by any means. But the CIA would never acknowledge they'd ever tasked them with missions. They wore generic uniforms and didn't carry identification or anything else associating them with the US government. If captured, they'd be completely disavowed by the organization they would to die for. Real *Mission Impossible* shit. Not surprising they were a tight group. As a SEAL, Logan knew that better than anyone. But putting a wall between yourself and the people supposed to cover your back was stupid at the best of times. On a mission like this one, nearly suicidal. Because, tonight, they snuck through the hilly, mountainous terrain of northeastern Syria, an area crawling with bad guys, looking for a Russian defector before someone else found and killed him.

The Russian pilot of a SU-24M attack aircraft had been shot down three days ago by the Turkish military for violating their airspace. The rest of the world thought the pilot already dead, killed by Kurdish militia troops as he'd parachuted to the ground. Instead, the Kurds had rescued him. According to their mission briefing, the entire thing had been an elaborate operation to get the Russian away from his people with a buttload of intelligence information in his possession. No one revealed the classified intel, but it must be damn good to go to all this trouble.

Logan had to admit, as escape plans went, this one was out there. The pilot, Nikolay Maksimov, had let the Kurds shoot a surface to air missile at his ass and hoped he—and his weapons officer, who had no idea Nikolay was defecting—survived. A Russian special ops team had picked up the weapons officer a few hours later. When the Russians didn't find Nikolay, the CIA hoped they would assume him dead. Instead, the Russians had somehow figured out his plan and flooded the area with their troops as well as their Syrian buddies. The SOG guys couldn't meet up with the Kurds to pick up Nikolay until the area cleared.

"We need to move," Joe said suddenly. "The Kurds holding our asset are getting antsy. They're going to bail if we don't meet them at rendezvous ASAP."

Logan shared a look with Chasen. Getting there without the bad guys seeing them would be hard as hell, but if they stayed in this ravine much longer, someone would stumble over them sooner rather than later.

He and Nash took point as they moved toward the small town of Roja toward the east, while Chasen and Dalton fell back to guard the rear.

They had to move slowly since most of the local fighters with them weren't wearing NVGs. Logan hadn't wanted them along on the mission, and not merely because they didn't have proper equipment, but, in the end, the CIA needed them to help keep all the allied factions working together during the exchange, especially the Kurds with the pilot.

They hadn't gone more than a hundred yards when Logan caught a flash of movement up near the crest of the ridge. He immediately signaled with his hand for everyone to find cover. Either the locals resisted to taking orders from an American or didn't like the idea of hiding because they didn't move fast enough.

Suddenly, automatic weapons fire shattered the stillness of the night. Two of the locals immediately went down. The Russians had found them.

Shit.

If Logan and his Team wanted to attack the Russians, they'd have to charge up the rocky slope, which didn't offer a hell of a lot of cover. Better to defend themselves from their current location. Unfortunately, the locals didn't like the idea any better and melted into the darkness even as Logan's Team and the CIA guys laid down weapon fire.

Then Joe arrived at Logan's side, shouting in his ear, "We need to pull back! The Kurds have bailed on the exchange and we have orders not to engage directly with the Russians!"

"It's a little fucking late," Logan pointed out as incoming bullets bounced off the rocks around him, throwing secondary fragments everywhere.

"You want to be the one responsible for starting World War III when Putin figures out Americans popped a few of his soldiers?" Joe asked.

Logan cursed silently. Definitely not the way he wanted to go down in the history books.

"Time to go," he said into the microphone on his headset keeping him in contact with his Team, as well as the SOG guys. "Exchange has been canceled."

Chasen didn't even look their way as he and Dalton tried to keep a group of Russians from coming down the far left end of the ridge and outflanking them. "What about the pilot?"

Joe answered. "We have to hope the Kurds can keep him alive long enough for us to arrange another pickup. Until then, he's on his own." He paused to return fire on more advancing Russians. "Right now, he's probably in a whole lot less crap than we are. Why don't you guys do some SEAL shit and get us the hell out of here?"

Logan chuckled as he motioned for his

Team to pull back and lay down cover fire. Maybe these SOG guys were all right. At least they had a sense of humor.

Chapter One

San Diego, California

FIGURE OUT A way to get onto the base or your sister dies."

The threating words kept replaying over and over in Felicia Bradford's head, freaking her out so badly her hands shook as she steered her SUV into a shopping center a mile from the gate of the Coronado Naval Amphibious Base and pulled into a space. Putting her Nissan Juke in park, she leaned forward and rested her forehead on the steering wheel. She wanted to cry, but she couldn't take the chance the people holding her sister would hear and think it meant she'd given up. They'd kill Stefanie for sure.

She took a deep breath and felt the tape holding the wire to her stomach pull a little, reminding her exactly where those horrible men had touched her as they'd attached the listening device to her skin. She shuddered at the thought her baby sister, a sophomore in college at the San Diego campus of the University of California, remained in their hands.

Felicia lifted her head and glanced at the clock on the dash. Two hours ago, she and Stef had been in their yoga class, something they did every Saturday morning at the same time. They'd been laughing and planning their next girls' night out when three men with accents had come out of nowhere and surrounded them in a quiet corner of the studio parking lot, taken Felicia's keys then hustled them into a white van at gunpoint.

The next ten minutes had been the most terrifying of her life as she and Stef sat huddled on the floor of the van while one of the men had kept his weapon trained on them the whole time. She'd feared the worst, thinking the men meant to rape and kill them, but when the van pulled into a warehouse and the doors opened, they dragged her and Stef into an office where they'd found two more men waiting. One tall and muscular with a buzz cut, the other not quite as tall or as muscled with long, shaggy hair. When Buzz Cut regarded Felicia and her sister like interesting bugs he'd seen crawling across the floor, a voice in the back of her head said this was a more complicated situation than she'd thought.

"What do you want with us?" she demanded, pushing her sister behind her.

Buzz Cut nodded at the men who'd

brought her and Stef into the room. A moment later, one of them jerked her sister away and forced her down into a chair then duct taped her wrists to the metal arms. Felicia tried to stop them, but the second man grabbed her before she could do much good.

"You are brave," Buzz Cut said in an Eastern European accent. At least she thought it was Eastern European. She wasn't very good with accents. "Good."

"What are you going to do with my sister?" Felicia demanded.

Buzz Cut crossed the room to stand in front of her. "I intend to kill your sister in the most painful way I can imagine unless you do exactly what I tell you.

Could someone so devoid of emotion be human? But the cold look in his eyes left Felicia with no doubt he told the truth.

"I'll do anything you want," she told him. "Just don't hurt her."

"Fortunately for you, what I need isn't very difficult. I want you to take something onto the Coronado Naval Amphibious Base for me and wait at a specific location for a short period of time then come back here. If you do, you and your sister may leave alive and unharmed."

Felicia almost started to hyperventilate. He made it sound so simple. "Coronado isn't open to the public. There's no way I can get on it."

His eyes narrowed. "The gate pass on the dash of your car says otherwise."

Crap. She'd forgotten she'd left it there. "It's from last weekend, but it's expired. I'm a wedding planner. I do a lot of weddings and receptions on the base."

"Then get it renewed," the man with the shaggy hair said.

Felicia looked at him. "It doesn't work like that. I have to arrange a separate gate pass for each wedding and someone with a military ID has to agree to be my sponsor."

Buzz Cut considered her statement. "How many times have you gone onto the station in the past six months?"

"I don't know. Maybe twenty-five or thirty times."

"With all those trips on base, are you trying to tell me a woman as attractive as you are couldn't make an impression on the guards? I'm sure you could talk your way through the gate this one time. Say it's for an emergency meeting with a client or something."

She opened her mouth to tell him she was nothing special—at least not special enough to get an MP or security guard to look the other way while she drove through the gate without a pass—but then she hesitated, knowing this asshole would kill her and Stef in a second if he decided she wasn't useful to him anymore. So, she'd nodded, telling him she could get on base.

The guy with the shaggy hair had then felt her up while taping the microphone wire to her stomach. When he finished, he and

Buzz Cut took her out to where her Nissan Juke waited beside the van. Then Buzz Cut had handed her a black plastic box about the size of a box of Kleenex along with a map of the NAB with a building circled in red.

"You need to be at this location no later than ten-thirty," Buzz Cut told her. "On the south side of the building is a picnic table under some palm trees. Sit at the table, turn on the machine, then wait there for exactly thirty minutes."

She tensed, terrified even to be in the same room with the box much less holding it. "Is this a bomb?"

"No. It's a listening device," he said. "It will record a conversation taking place nearby. No one will be hurt."

Felicia didn't believe him. "If that's all, why don't you have one of your men take it on base? I'm sure there are lots of people who could do a much better job than me."

Mouth tight, Buzz Cut jerked the box and the map away from her and handed it to Shaggy Hair. Felicia's heart fell into her stomach as he grabbed her arm and hauled her across the warehouse to another office, then shoved her inside. She tripped over something on the floor, falling half on top of it. She pushed herself up and almost screamed when she realized it was a man in a Navy uniform, the front of his blue camouflage top soaked with blood. He stared unseeingly up at the ceiling.

She scrambled off the man as Buzz Cut

jerked her to her feet.

"This is the man I got to do the job, but he had a change of heart at the last minute, and I had to kill him." Cold, dark eyes bore into hers. "Don't make me have to find someone else to do this job. The time window I have to get it done is small and, if you make me miss it, I'll take it out on your precious sister."

She didn't say anything as he led her back out to her SUV, which one of the men must have driven here from the shopping center, and shoved her behind the wheel. She thought she'd been as freaked out as she could be when Shaggy Hair leaned in and put a handgun in the center console.

"Why are you giving that to me?" she asked.

Buzz Cut shrugged. "If things don't go the way you plan, you'll need to improvise if you want your sister to live. If it means you have to shoot someone, do it."

Felicia couldn't kill someone in cold blood. But, to save her sister, maybe she could.

They took her phone out of her purse and wrote down her phone number.

"In case I want to contact you," Buzz Cut said as he handed it back to her. "Don't get any brilliant ideas about calling the police. With the wire you're wearing, we'll be able to hear everything you say, and if you say something you shouldn't, I'll kill your sister. If you don't get to the location on the map in time, I'll kill your sister. If you don't get us what we want and come straight back here, I'll kill your sister. And if we suddenly lose the audio from the wire. I'll kill your sister."

Felicia had been so shaken by images of her sister being tortured and killed, she could barely drive across the Coronado Bridge to the base. She'd raised Stef ever since their parents died six years ago. The idea of something bad happening to her made it hard even to breathe. She had no doubt Buzz Cut would kill Stef if she didn't show up with the information they wanted. He might kill both of them anyway once he had what he wanted, of course, but she could deal with only one problem at a time.

Unfortunately, as she'd expected, the guards at the gate refused to let her through, no matter how much she tried to sweet talk them. She batted her eyes and tried to convince one particular MP on duty who'd flirted with her on several occasions she had to get on base for a few minutes to scout out the location for an upcoming wedding, but the guy hadn't budged.

She'd turned around and been driving away from the base when her phone rang.

"Figure out a way to get on base," Buzz Cut ordered. "Or your sister dies."

Felicia continued to stare at the clock on the dash as it slowly counted down the minutes. She had twenty-nine minutes left. She needed to figure out something or Stef would be dead.

In frustration, she reached into the center console and pulled out the weapon stashed there. She didn't even have a clue how to fire a gun, but maybe she could use it to threaten her way through the gate. Then what? The military police would chase her once she got on base.

Felicia caught sight of a group of men and women in Navy uniforms coming out of the grocery store. An idea hit her. Insane and probably wouldn't work, but the only thing she could think of was shoving her gun in the nearest sailor's back and demanding he or she help her get on base. She only prayed she'd find a sailor who didn't have a hero complex. She really didn't want to have to shoot anyone—even if she could figure out how to do it. But, when it came to her sister, she'd do what she had to do.

Felicia turned off the engine and waited. It would probably be smarter to scope out the possible targets and pick someone smaller and preferably female, but as the clock on the dash continued to get closer to the ten-thirty deadline, she realized she didn't have time

She shoved the gun and the black box into her purse then got out and walked over to the store. The first few sailors came out in groups of two and three. Dammit, she didn't have time for this!

Then she spotted a hunky, dark-haired guy in blue camouflage coming her way, a couple of grocery bags in his hands—alone.

Also at least a foot taller than her and probably outweighed her by a hundred pounds. Her gut told her this guy wasn't the best choice, but she couldn't wait any longer.

Heart pounding in her chest and a hand on the gun in her purse, she turned and followed, hurrying to catch up with him. When they got close to his blue SUV, she pulled the gun out of her purse, closed the distance between them, and shoved the weapon in his back. He immediately stopped in his tracks.

"I don't want to shoot you, but I will if you don't help me get on base," she said as firmly as she could. The words didn't sound as intimidating as she'd hoped, but at least her voice hadn't squeaked.

She didn't know what to expect, but when the big man didn't move at all, she got a little nervous.

"Don't do anything foolish or you'll be putting the lives of innocent people in danger," she warned. "I've never fired a gun before, and if you make me do it now, I have no idea where the bullets are going to go."

The guy still didn't move. But at least he didn't spin around and try to disarm her. Unfortunately, the seconds continued to fly past, bringing Stefanie's death ever closer. Felicia might have to do something else—although she didn't know what—to prove her seriousness. Could she whack him in the back of the head? Probably not without making the gun go off. Then what? Unconscious, he wouldn't be able to get her on base.

"Did you hear what I said?" she prompted, shoving the gun more firmly into his back.

"I heard you," he said. "Relax, okay? There's no need to pull the trigger. I'll get you on base. But I want your word you won't hurt anyone if I do."

She couldn't believe he tried to bargain with her when she had a gun pointed at him. "It's the last thing I want."

He lifted his right hand, and Felicia tensed, until she realized he was only lifting the key fob for his SUV. He unlocked the doors with a *beep-beep* then opened the driver's side. Felicia wondered if she should let him drive or if she should do it. After a moment, she decided the guards on the gate would never let them through with her behind the wheel, so it had to be him. But she couldn't tell him to wait while she ran around to the passenger side, either.

Finally, she climbed into the SUV first and crawled over the center console to get into the passenger seat, keeping the weapon pointed at him the whole time.

"Get in," she ordered. "And don't try anything."

As he climbed in, she saw the name Dunn embroidered on a tag on his uniform. Nice name. It fit him.

She was wondering about his first name when she finally got a good look at his face. She couldn't see his eyes because he wore aviators, but with a chiseled jaw and wide, sensual mouth, he was way more handsome than any man had a right to be. She hoped he did what she told him. She'd feel horrible shooting someone so attractive.

Okay, absolutely the dumbest thought she'd ever had. Would she feel better shooting him if he were ugly?

Dunn reached around to put his grocery bags on the floorboard in the back then fastened his seatbelt. When he finished, he lifted a brow. "You going to put on your seatbelt?"

Felicia's jaw may have dropped. Seriously? Obviously, he wouldn't even start the vehicle until she buckled up. Unfortunately, she couldn't get her belt on while holding a pistol. She glanced around for a place to put it, figuring wedging it between her legs wasn't the best idea. She finally ended up putting it on the floor. The moment she had her seatbelt on, she reached down and snatched it up with trembling hands, turning to point it in Dunn's direction.

He regarded her with a look plainly suggesting he knew this was her first foray into taking a hostage, but he thankfully didn't say it out loud. Instead, he cranked the SUV and headed out of the parking lot.

"I hope this doesn't take too long," he remarked as he drove toward the Naval Amphibious Base. "I bought ice cream and would hate to have to throw it away if it melts."

Felicia didn't know what to say. How

the hell could the man be so calm when he had a gun pointed at him?

As they neared the gate, Logan reached into his back pocket for his wallet and pulled out his ID card. She slipped the gun in her purse.

"Don't make me hurt anyone," she said him.

"I told you I'd get you on base and I will," Dunn said as he weaved through the barricades put there to slow people down. "Keep the gun in your purse and everything will be fine."

Dunn had a very trustworthy-looking face and Felicia wanted to believe him, but she still tensed when they rolled to a stop beside the guard at the gate. At least it wasn't the cute MP she'd tried to sweet-talk earlier. In fact, she didn't recognize the older guy at all.

"Dunn, my man," the guard said. "I haven't seen you in weeks. How the hell are you?"

"I'm good," Dunn said conversationally. "How about you?

"Can't complain." The guard leaned down and regarded Felicia. "Who's this? New girlfriend?"

Crap. She hadn't thought about having a cover story. Passing her off as a girlfriend might work, though.

Dunn chuckled. "Nah. This is my sister Claire. She's staying with me for a while, and I'm showing her around. I'm going to get her a base access on Monday."

The older man smiled and nodded. "No problem."

While they'd made it this far, Felicia refused to let herself exhale until the guard waved them through the gate. She glanced at the clock on the dash, comparing it with her watch. Ten minutes.

"Drive faster," she said, pulling out the gun so she could point it at him and the map so she could figure out where she needed to go.

"If I drive over the speed limit, there's a good chance we'll get pulled over."

"If you drive under the speed limit, there's a good chance someone very important to me will die," she told him. "So, drive faster."

Dunn looked at her sharply. She expected him to say something, but instead he drove faster.

"Where are we going?" he asked softly.

Her knowledge of NAB Coronado limited to the location of the church and the various clubs that held receptions, she held the map up for him to see and pointed at the part circled in red.

"Right there," she said. "And I have to be there in five minutes."

He studied the circled area on the map for a moment then gave her another intense look. "You sure you want to go there?"

The spot on the map probably had some significance to him, but to her, it was simply the place Buzz Cut told to be—in five minutes.

"Yes."

As Dunn turned down a side road and picked up speed, Felicia held out hope this might work. She wasn't naive. She knew the men holding Stef couldn't be trusted. But she had to believe if she did as Buzz Cut told her, maybe everything would work out okay. It was the only thing she had to hang onto until something better came along.

"We didn't have a chance for a proper introduction, but my name's Logan," he said. "What's yours?"

Felicia ignored him, or tried to, anyway, but he kept talking in a frustratingly calm, casual voice.

"Maybe I can help you out of your situation," he continued. "You don't really seem to be the kind of person to do something like this."

She wasn't. But she was doing it now—for Stefanie.

"Keep driving," she told him.

Felicia hadn't realized they'd reached their destination until Logan pulled the SUV into a parking space and turned off the engine. Off to one side of the large official-looking building a sign read *Naval Special Warfare Command*.

She looked around, trying to remember exactly where Buzz Cut had told her to take the box.

"Where's the south side of the

building?" she asked.

Logan pointed to the right.

She pulled the box out of her purse then motioned at Logan with the weapon. "Get out and walk in front of me to the picnic table over there. The gun will be in my purse, but I'll have my finger on the trigger the whole time, so don't try anything."

His gaze locked on the box in her hand. "What's that?"

The dash clock read ten twenty-nine.

"I can't tell you anything, so stop asking me questions and get out," she snapped.

He regarded her silently for a moment then shut off the engine and got out of the SUV. She climbed over the console and followed him to the south side of the building.

The table stood right where Buzz Cut said it would be, under some palm trees. The moment she and Logan sat down, she put the box on the table and turned the lone switch on the top until she heard a clicking sound. She kept turning it until it stopped moving. Then she sat there staring at the box—and Logan.

He took of his sunglasses, revealing gorgeous blue eyes, then reached into his pocket for his cellphone.

"What are you doing?" she asked nervously, fumbling for the gun in her purse and pointing it at him.

"Playing a game on my phone." He shrugged. "I figure we're going to be sitting here a while, aren't we?"

She frowned. He clicked way too many keys for any game. Was he calling the cops? She didn't want to have to shoot him, but he might not give her a choice.

But then he turned the phone around to show her what he'd typed.

I know you can't talk, but I can help you if you'll let me. Tell me what's going on.

Felicia blinked. How had he figured out she couldn't talk?

He nodded at her, then pointed at the words he'd written on his phone, specifically the part where he'd said he could help her.

A thousand thoughts raced through her head. Could she trust him? Could he really help her? She couldn't imagine how he could, but she needed help from someone, and her instincts told her Dunn was that person.

Reaching down, she lifted the hem of her tank top, exposing her stomach and the wire taped there.

Logan leaned in close, followed the wire around to the little square thing taped to her lower back, and nodded. Sitting back, he typed something else into his phone, then held it up so she could see.

Do you have a cellphone?

Chapter Two

LOGAN HAD ONLY gone into work beaucoup early on his day off because he had to finish up some paperwork from the mission in Syria. Next, his plan had been to veg out in front of the TV watching cheesy sci-fi movies and eating junk food for two whole days. But then a beautiful woman had stepped up behind him as he came out of the grocery store and shoved a gun in his back, and his weekend plans had changed.

He could tell right from the get-go she didn't have a clue how to handle a gun. Not only was the safety on her Sig Sauer 9mm on, but she shook like a leaf the whole time she had it pointed at him. That alone told him neither he nor anyone else was in immediate danger. Why did she want to get on base so badly? From the way she'd looked at the clock every other minute, she had some kind of timetable.

When she pointed at the spot on the

map, Logan realized the seriousness of the situation. She wanted to go to the headquarters building of the Navy Special Warfare Command from which the Navy ran its special operation missions—and where his bosses from SEAL Team 5 worked. If she wanted to go there, it was because there was something big happening.

If she hadn't been wearing a snug-fitting tank top and yoga pants with those wide-leg bottoms, he would have thought her a suicide bomber. Hell, with her long, dark hair up in a ponytail and a hint of makeup, she looked like the girl next door. But while she had plenty of curves under her outfit, none of them were explosive—at least not in the literal sense. And he was pretty sure the black box wasn't a bomb either.

He could have disarmed her a dozen times over already, but instead he went with his gut and took her where she wanted to go. His instincts had gotten him out of one bad situation after another over the years, and right now, his gut told him she was in serious trouble.

He couldn't help her if he didn't know what the hell was going on though. Something about the way she refused to answer his questions made him think there she couldn't talk. So he'd pulled out his cellphone. The relief on her face when she thought he truly might be able to help her made his heart squeeze. When she'd lifted the hem of her tank top and shown him the quality surveillance gear taped to her sexy belly, he knew his gut had been right. She was in trouble and she needed his help.

Hands shaking, she took her phone out of her purse and handed it to him. He took it and put his name and number in her contacts, then turned off the ringer and gave it back to her.

Setting his own phone to silence, he texted his first question. *What's your name?*

She pushed up her sunglasses to see the screen better, then texted him back. *Felicia.*

Nice name. Okay, now for the serious question. *Is someone close to you in danger?*

She read the message on her phone then started typing furiously.

Five men with heavy accents grabbed my sister and me this morning. They gave me the box and told me to come to this building and turn it on then stay here for 30 minutes or they'd kill my sister.

Were they armed? he texted back.

She nodded and went back to typing. Damn, she had fast fingers.

Four of them carrying pistols. I assume the fifth one—their leader—has one, too, but I never saw it. They gave me the pistol in my purse in case things went wrong, but I don't want to hurt anyone.

He smiled. He couldn't imagine someone like Felicia ever wanting to hurt anyone. But she'd done what was necessary to try and help her sister. He could respect that.

Do you know what this box is?

She stared at the thing on the table for a moment before answering. *The leader—a really big guy with a military style haircut—said it's a listening device. He had a sailor to do the job, but he tried to back out so they killed him. They want me to bring the box back to them after I'm done here.*

The fact one person was already dead wasn't good, but everything else she'd said pretty much lined up with what Logan had thought earlier. This box was somehow recording the meeting going on in the NSWC building, even though it should have been frigging impossible with all the security precautions put into place by Navy security. You couldn't walk into any secured building on this base—or any other—with a cellphone, iPad, e-reader, Apple Watch, thumb drive, or even a Fitbit. Nothing electronic went into a facility where they were discussing classified information, like the Special Warfare headquarters.

He had no doubt someone had gotten a microphone of some type in there. This black box sure as hell wasn't picking up conversations all the way out here. He didn't care what kind of technology it used.

On the upside, at least the thing wasn't a repeater box—something that picked up the signal from inside the building and transferred it off the base wirelessly. The fact the men wanted Felicia to bring it back to them suggested it was nothing more than a recorder. He hoped to hell he was right or these assholes would get away with a buttload of classified information.

Logan was tempted to reach over and turn off the listening device, but he resisted. He had no way of knowing if they had something in the box that might signal them if it he did. Better to leave it on and make sure the people holding Felicia's sister hostage never got their hands on it.

Do you know the address of the place they want you to bring the box?

Felicia gave him a vague answer. The warehouse was off Trentham Way in Poway, but she didn't know a specific address.

That was okay. She got him close with a description. That was good enough. But when he started typing into his phone again, Felicia reached out a hand to stop him. Then she frantically typed into her phone. A moment later, he got a text written in all caps.

YOU CAN'T CALL THE COPS! THEY'LL GET STEFANIE KILLED!

Logan understood Felicia's concern. She was probably right. The cops would surround the place per standard operating procedure and Felicia's sister would likely end up dead. But calling the cops had never been his intent.

I'm not texting the cops. I'm texting a few friends of mine. They'll help me get your sister out of there. I swear it.

She studied him for a moment, and he could see the fear and hope warring with each other in her beautiful brown eyes.

You can get my sister out safely?

Logan reached out and grabbed her hand, then looking her deep in the eyes, he nodded before texting her back.

Saving people in danger is what I've spend most of my adult live either training for, or doing. If you trust me, we can get your sister out.

Felicia hesitated, but then she finally nodded. *Okay.*

Logan knew Felicia trusted him with the most important thing in the world to her. He wouldn't let her down.

He fired off a text to a couple of guys on the Team, telling them he needed help and giving them the basics of the situation. He focused on the tactical details as he knew them. A warehouse in the Poway industrial area, five bad guys, one hostage, handguns for weapons, and a willingness to kill when necessary. Lastly he told them what his basic plan would be. If they didn't make it there in time, he'd be going in anyway.

I'll be there, was the unanimous answer.

Logan spent the next few minutes asking Felicia for as much detail of the warehouse's layout as she could remember. Locations of doors and windows, the room Stefanie was in, if the men were right-handed or left-handed—anything and everything

Felicia could think of. In between texting, he kept up a stream of meaningless verbal crap to make sure the people on the other end of Felicia's wire knew they were still there and everything was going according to plan.

When the thirty minutes were up, Felicia turned off the box and told him to go back to the car, reminding him to not do anything stupid or she'd shoot him. When they got in his SUV, she handed the gun to him. He dropped the clip and checked the chamber to make sure it was loaded. It was. The bad guys must have believed she'd do anything necessary to save her sister. It'd be nice shoving this same gun up their asses.

They'd left base and were crossing back over the bridge into San Diego when Felicia's phone rang. She took a deep breath and then answered it.

"Yes, I have the box with me," she told the person on the other end of the line. "I'll be there in ten minutes. Is my sister okay?"

Whatever the guy on the phone said, it mustn't have satisfied Felicia because he saw her mouth tighten.

"I want to talk to her," she demanded.

Logan expected the other person to argue, but instead, Felicia sagged with relief.

"Are you okay, Stef? Have they hurt you?"

The bad guys didn't give her sister very long to talk because a moment later, Felicia stiffened.

"Yes," she said. "I know what I have to

do."

She hung up and typed something into her phone when they got the next red light, then showed it to him.

He wants me to take your cellphone then get rid of you.

Logan nodded and texted back. *Tell me to stop once we get off I-15 at Scripps Parkway.*

Fifteen minutes later, Felicia ordered him to stop the SUV and get out. He made a pretense of resisting, just as she made a pretense of saying she'd shoot him. While he got out to slip into the back so he could lie down on the floorboard, Felicia climbed over the console to take the wheel. A minute later, they headed east on the Scripps-Poway Parkway toward the warehouse.

He thumbed out a quick text then held his phone up so she could see it. *When you're about a block or two away, slow down so I can hop out.*

Felicia threw him a look over her shoulder but then nodded.

He was checking on the status of his SEAL Teammates when Felicia coughed softly and slowed down. Logan shoved his phone in his pocket then opened the door and rolled out. He landed in the grass along the side of the road, bouncing a couple of times before coming to a stop in the ditch. All in all, not a bad landing. He'd hit harder coming in on a parachute with a heavy combat load.

He looked around, careful to stay low

to the ground. This part of the Poway industrial district was relatively quiet on the weekend, which was good. Seeing him roll out of a moving vehicle might encourage people to call the cops.

Taking the gun from his waistband, he watched as Felicia slowed the SUV even more then turned down a side street two blocks up the road. He figured out which warehouse she was heading for then sprinted for the one adjacent to it. He wanted to get to some cover fast, find his guys, then move on the warehouse. If his instincts were right, the men holding Felicia's sister would kill both of them the moment they confirmed she had what they wanted.

He made it to the far side of the building adjacent to the warehouse where Felicia stopped then waited.

She got out of the vehicle slowly, taking her time to reach in and get the black box. Good. She was giving him time to get into position.

As Logan darted across the space between the two warehouses, he thought he might have to do this raid on his own since he'd yet to find his guys, or even hear from them. But, when he edged around the side of the warehouse, he found Nash and Dalton coming toward him with Glocks in hand.

"Shit, it took you long enough to get here," Nash said. "We thought we'd have to go in and get the girl on our own."

"Stef still okay?" Logan asked as he led

his men around the back of the warehouse.

"So far, but those guys are getting antsy in there," Dalton said in that Southern drawl of his. "One of them left about ten minutes ago, so we're down to four."

Logan nodded. He didn't like the idea one of them had gotten away, but it made for better odds for everyone involved.

He glanced over his shoulder at Nash and Dalton. "What's with the shorts and T-shirts. Some kind of SoCal tactical outfit?"

Nash shrugged. A couple of years younger than Logan, he was the Team's resident medic. "You caught us at the beach, and we figured we didn't have time to go home and change."

"Okay, but if you were at the beach, where did the hardware come from?" Logan darted another quick look behind him. "Don't tell me you two have started carrying weapons around in your vehicles?"

Dalton snorted. "No, but after all the crap that went down with Nesbitt a couple of months ago, would you blame us?"

Logan couldn't argue with that logic. Nesbitt had been a crooked city councilman Chasen had gotten into a scuffle with. The whole thing had ended with Logan sneaking onto Nesbitt's property with Chasen, Nash, and Dalton and conducting a little armed reconnaissance. To say things had gotten a bit messy was putting it mildly.

"Chasen brought them with him. They're fully registered and legal," Nash said.

"Let's hope we don't have to shoot anyone, or he's never going to get them back."

Hopefully, no one would get shot today. "Where's Chasen now?"

"Around back," Dalton whispered. "He wanted to stay close to the door in case things escalated in there."

Chasen stood with his back to the warehouse, his gun down at his side but at the ready. Unlike Nash and Dalton, he mustn't have been at the beach because he wore jeans and a T-shirt. Two years older than Logan, he'd been his swim buddy in BUD/s.

"We don't have a lot of time to waste on fancy planning," Chasen said, the East Coast accent he'd come into BUD/s with all but gone. "Your girl won't give them the box unless they release her sister, and they won't release her until she gives up the box."

Shit.

"Then we won't waste time," Logan said. "Chasen, you and Nash take the left. Dalton and I will take the right. Try to bring in these guys alive, if you can, but don't hesitate to shoot if you have to."

Giving them a nod, Logan led the way to the back door. Once there, he lifted a hand, silently counting down with his fingers.

Four...three...two...one.

When he got to one, he kicked in the back door as hard as he could. It flew back and slammed into the wall as he and the other guys darted inside. A huge garage door was at the far end and offices lined the right wall.

Felicia stood in the center of the warehouse opposite a big guy with wild hair, the box clutched in her hands. Three other men stood off to the side, guns casually down at their sides. Logan didn't see Stefanie at all.

At their entrance, Felicia and the men spun around to face them, guns automatically coming up.

"Drop the guns," Logan ordered.

The three armed men hesitated, as if unsure whether to comply or not. The guy with the unkempt hair wasn't so slow to action. Pulling a gun from behind his back, he strode toward one of the side offices.

Stefanie.

Logan aimed the Sig Sauer, intending to put the guy down before he moved another step, when Felicia suddenly darted after the man. Cursing, Logan pulled up, forced to forego the shot or risk hitting her.

He charged forward, hoping to get a better angle on the man—or just fucking tackle him if he had to. But when he got close, the guy spun around and caught Felicia's arm, shoving her in Logan's direction.

Logan sidestepped her, but it didn't matter. The man slid to a halt beside Stefanie. She was tied to a metal chair, dark eyes so similar to Felicia's filled with terror.

Smiling at Logan, the guy with the wild hair and the eyes to match put the gun to Stefanie's head. He had to know if he pulled the trigger he'd die, too. He simply didn't seem to care—as long as he could take Felicia's sister with him.

"No!" Felicia screamed.

Logan snapped his pistol up in a rapid fire drill he'd practiced hundreds—maybe thousands—of times. He didn't set his feet; he didn't square his shoulders. Hell, he didn't even aim. He merely let the barrel instinctively follow his eyes and pulled the trigger.

The hole in the psycho's forehead was amazingly small, but experience told Logan the one coming out the back was much bigger. Blood painted the back wall of the little office then the man fell, gun slipping from his lifeless fingers.

Even though Logan didn't hear any other shooting, he still spun around, wanting to make sure his Teammates were okay. Chasen, Nash, and Dalton were each trussing up a bad guy with his own shoestrings.

Felicia brushed past him, running into the office to throw her arms around her sister, crying like crazy as she tore at the grey tape holding the girl to the chair.

Logan walked into the office and placed the 9mm on the desk. Looking at the two sisters embrace, he liked to think this screwed-up day was finally over with, but he knew it was only getting started.

Chapter Three

THE POLICE TOOK the three surviving kidnappers away first then put up crime tape across the doors of the office where the dead sailor had been as well as the one where Logan had shot the guy with the shaggy hair. Then the cops started asking questions—lots of questions.

Felicia thought she'd done fairly well answering them, and Stef held up like a trouper. She'd started thinking maybe she and her sister would make it home by dinner. She didn't feel like eating anything after the day she'd had, but it would be nice to have a little time to herself to decompress from everything. Then the men and women in suits showed up, and the questioning took on a whole different tone.

They flashed a lot of badges and ID's in her face, most of which she forgot within moments. But she recognized the acronyms—FBI, CIA, NSA, DHS, even NCIS. She'd been so sure Hollywood had fabricated the last organization purely for TV. Apparently not.

It wasn't until they began asking her and Stef the same questions over and over that Felicia realized they thought she and her sister were involved in this.

Do you know why they grabbed you and your sister in particular? Why didn't you call the police? Why didn't you tell the guards at the gate they were holding your sister hostage? Did you know what was in the black box? Have you ever met LPO Dunn before? Did you have a prior relationship with any of the men who allegedly held you and your sister hostage? Have you ever met the dead sailor in the warehouse? Who decided to call in the other Navy personnel instead of the police?

After two solid hours of being interrogated, Felicia felt like she might lose it. She wasn't sure if it meant smacking someone or breaking down into tears, but just when it seemed she couldn't handle one more asinine question, she felt an arm wrap around her shoulders. She looked up to find Logan there.

"I think that's enough questions," he said.

Most of the federal agents, especially the ones from the FBI and DHS took offense to him interfering, but when Logan mentioned Russia and Syria, the conversation came to a screeching halt. That probably had something to do with the CIA and NSA announcing this case had wandered into classified areas out of the purview of the other parties involved. Five minutes later, the CIA herded her, Stefanie, and Logan outside to a black SUV and drove them straight back to NAB Coronado.

When they got to the building with a sign out front saying Force Protection, the CIA agents led them to a conference room where they got her, Stef, and Logan coffee and offered them something to eat. The questioning continued, but unlike before, no one seemed to be accusing her or her sister of doing anything illegal. Probably because Logan was sitting right beside Felicia with a look on his handsome face that said he'd punch the next person who dared to piss him off. Felicia couldn't put into words how good it was having him there. He'd already saved her sister's life, and now he'd saved Felicia's sanity.

A little while later, an artist showed up with a computerized sketchpad and came up with a 3D image d eerily close to the scary guy who'd threatened to kill her and Stef. While most of the agents disappeared to start working on identifying Buzz Cut—who'd taken off before Felicia had gotten back to the warehouse—a few of them stayed behind to talk to see if Stef overheard anything while she'd been held captive that would clue them in to where Buzz Cut might be or who he worked for.

Felicia wanted to stay and support her sister, but after thirty more minutes of seemingly endless questions, the adrenaline she'd been running on since morning finally ran out.

In between questions, she gave Stef's hand a squeeze. "I'm going to stretch my legs. I'll be right back."

The hallway was empty, but in the room across from her the CIA agents were looking at video footage on a TV monitor. She couldn't hear everything they said, but she picked up a few words. Mostly it was stuff about Syria and the fighting going on over there, and meetings between the CIA and the Navy. If Felicia were the curious type, she would have been tempted to eavesdrop. As it was, none of it made a bit of sense to her. Even if it had, she was too tired to care.

"You holding up okay?" Logan asked from behind her.

She turned, giving him a small smile. "Yeah, thanks to you. Speaking of which, I never did get a chance to thank you."

His mouth edged up. "I'm pretty sure anyone would have done the same thing given the chance."

Felicia seriously doubted that but didn't bother to point it out. Something told her Logan was too humble for that. "Well, thanks, regardless. I owe you more than I can ever repay, not only for what you did for me, but for Stef, too. The man you shot would have killed her."

Logan frowned. "I'm sorry he got as close as he did. I hoped to stop him before he got anywhere near her."

"You stopped him when it mattered. That's all I care about," she said. "You aren't going to get into any trouble for shooting him, are you?"

Logan shook his head. "I don't think so. No one has brought it up, and I'm not going to worry about it until they do."

She'd worry for him. In her opinion, Logan hadn't done anything wrong, but that didn't mean the authorities—or the Navy— would feel the same way. "What about your friends?"

"As far as the police are concerned, they happened to be in the right place at the right time."

Felicia had a handful of good friends, but if she sent them a quick text saying she needed them to come to a warehouse in the middle of nowhere armed with weapons, she doubted she'd get many replies. Logan's buddies were as incredible as he was. Not as good looking, maybe—at least, in her opinion—but definitely brave and loyal as hell.

Before she could say anything, one of the CIA agents—Jonathan Olson—came out of the room across the hall, a tablet computer in his hand. He held it up in front of Felicia. "Is this the guy who ran the show?"

She looked down at the picture of the man. It was a photo from a traffic cam, but even with the reflection off the windshield, she recognized Buzz Cut. She'd never forget his face.

"It's him," she said. I can't believe you found him already."

Olson snorted. "We found him all right. This picture was taken at the San Ysidro border crossing into Mexico two hours ago. He's probably sixty miles on the other side of Tijuana by now." His mouth tightened. "Which may actually be the best possible outcome, as far as you're concerned, Petty Officer Dunn."

Logan's eyes narrowed. "What do you mean by that?"

Olson pointed to the tablet. "I mean this guy—Illarion Volkov—is one nasty SOB. He served in both Russian Special Forces and their Foreign Intel Service, but they considered him so out of control they not only tossed him out of the military and covert intelligence communities, but out of Russia, too. There are a lot of rumors swirling around as to why, but apparently he showed a willingness to kill a whole lot of people in his efforts to accomplish his missions. Since being exiled, he's been working as a mercenary for anyone who will hire him, which includes Russia, as strange as that is."

"He sounds like the kind of man the CIA would have wanted to get their hands on," Logan said.

"We do," Olson agreed. "But considering you killed his brother, it's probably a good thing he took off."

Felicia's stomach clenched. "You don't think he'll come back, do you?"

The mere thought of him coming after

her and Stef—or Logan—made her feel like she might pass out.

Olson shook his head. "It's not likely. Sure, he'll be pissed about his brother, but he's also smart enough to know he was lucky to get away as it is. He's not dumb enough to try to slip back into the US, not purely based on a need for revenge."

Felicia hoped he was right.

Olson glanced at the conference room. "We're almost done with your sister. You should be able to go home in a little while."

His idea of a little while turned out to be another hour, but at least Logan hung around with Felicia while they waited. Now she and Stef were safe, she could fully appreciate how gorgeous he was. Not to mention what a nice guy he was. She didn't know if it was because they'd gone through a life-and-death experience together, but standing there in the hallway talking about inconsequential everyday things, she felt like she'd known him for years.

"You want a ride back to the grocery store where you left your car?" Logan asked after the CIA finally finished up with Stef. When Felicia gave him a questioning look, he added, "One of my buddies drove my SUV over here from the warehouse."

She hadn't even thought about his SUV—or hers—until now. "In that case, yes. If it's not too much trouble."

It hadn't sounded nearly as ridiculous when she said it in her head. Like she hadn't caused him enough already by taking his hostage.

But Logan smiled. "No trouble at all."

They didn't say much on the way back to the shopping center. Probably because they were all tired. Heck, Stef looked like she might nod off in the backseat. Felicia couldn't blame her. It had been one hell of a day. She was just glad her sister was okay.

Felicia turned around to face front again when she caught sight of the grocery bags on the floorboard.

"Crap," she said, looking at Logan. "You have ice cream back there."

"Damn. I completely forgot about it." He cringed. "It's probably a big gooey mess. The hot dogs probably didn't fare so well either."

She blinked. "You eat hot dogs?"

Even wearing a uniform, she could tell how built he was. The urge to reach out and squeeze his biceps to see if she was right was so strong, she practically had to sit on her hands to keep from giving in.

Luckily, Logan didn't seem to notice. Instead, he gave her an injured look. "What's wrong with hot dogs?"

"Nothing, I suppose," she said. "I assumed you'd be more of a lean protein guy."

He let out a chuckle. "Lean protein means cooking, and cooking's above my pay grade. Unless it's in a microwave. I can handle that."

She laughed. She still couldn't understand how he could have a body like his on a diet of hot dogs and Hot Pockets. The image gave her an idea though.

"I figured out how to repay you for what you did for Stef and me," she said. "I'm going to make you dinner."

In reality, it didn't even begin to cover what she owed him. She wasn't sure if anything ever could. But a home-cooked meal was the least she could do.

"You don't have to do that," he insisted. "I don't expect anything in return for today."

He was humble, all right. It was a quality that made him even more attractive.

"I know," she said. "But I want to."

Logan flashed her a smile as he turned into the parking lot of the shopping center. "Okay, sounds good."

Felicia relaxed in her seat, relieved—and more than a little thrilled—he'd accepted her invitation. She would have asked him to follow her back to her place right then, but that meant bailing on her sister, and she wanted to spend some time with Stef to make sure she was okay after what happened today.

"Next Friday work for you?" she asked Logan.

"Definitely." He glanced at her, his mouth curving into a sexy grin and making her pulse skip a beat. "I can't wait."

She smiled. "Me, either."

Chapter Four

IS THE OLD man still pissed at you?"

Logan didn't answer Nash's question. Mostly because carrying on a conversation while wearing a gas mask was hard as hell. Then again, crawling on your belly through the mud beneath a barbed wire-covered obstacle while wearing the heavy rubber contraption was damn difficult, too. But that was the whole point. To make the Monster Mash even more challenging.

The Monster Mash was a combination of physical and skills training. This particular session had started at 0500 that morning, and Logan and his Team were still going strong three hours later.

The event had started off with a two-mile swim in the ocean followed by a six-mile run along the sandy beach. After that, they'd done a series of training events, which included everything from doing first aid on "patients" who'd been shot or hit with fragments from an IED to putting together a satellite communication kit so they could call in a medevac helicopter for the wounded, then doing maintenance on some broken AK-47 assault rifles until fully functional so they could subsequently secure the landing zone for the bird. As usual, getting from one event to the next required a lot of running while carrying a load of gear at the same time.

The second to last stage was the gas mask obstacle course. Once done, it would be another run along the beach, where they'd get picked up by a boat and hauled back to base.

The Monster Mash made for an exhausting morning, but there was no better way to train. If you could do basic tasks like first aid, equipment operation, and weapon maintenance while you were dog tired, there was a good chance you'd be able to do it in combat.

Logan ripped off his gas mask the second he came out from underneath the barbed wire and shoved it in the pouch on his hip.

"Yeah, Commander Hunt is still steamed," Logan said as he fell into a run alongside Nash. "The old man raked me over the coals the last two days."

When Logan hadn't been with the CIA, NSA, and Naval Intelligence. He'd spent Monday and Tuesday at the headquarters building, and this was his first day back with his Team's platoon.

"What'd you tell him?" Dalton asked from the other side of Logan as they ran. "I mean, beyond the obvious fact you were befuddled by a beautiful woman pulling a gun on you?"

Logan chuckled. "I was smart enough to not bring that up. I chose to go with a more common *I thought I did the right thing*."

"Did he buy it?"

"Not really." Logan snorted. "I swear the guy hasn't done a damn thing that wasn't by the book."

On the other side of Nash, Chasen laughed. "I don't know. I remember Kurt telling me some stories about Hunt. According to him, the guy used to be a hell raiser back when he was a lieutenant."

Logan found that hard to believe, even if the platoon's senior enlisted member Chief Kurt Travers had been the one telling those stories. Logan was sure if he checked, he'd find a stick up Mack Hunt's ass.

"What did the feds want to talk about?" Nash asked. "I would have thought they'd have all their answers from the hours they spent questioning you and those two women on Saturday."

"I thought so, too," Logan agreed. "But they kept going over what happened. They asked a lot of questions about our mission over in Syria, too."

Chasen looked at him sharply. "What did you tell them?"

"Nothing at first since I didn't know if I

could," Logan admitted. "But Hunt told me to spill the beans about everything."

The guys did a collective double take. SEALs rarely talked about what they did on their missions, even with the CIA and NSA.

"You can't tell me the Russians forcing a woman to bring a recording device onto base isn't related to the pilot we were there to rescue," Chasen said.

"Yeah, no kidding," Logan said. "No one would say it in so many words, but from the whispers I heard, the CIA and US Special Operations Command were meeting in the NSWC building on Saturday to discuss how badly everyone wants to get their hands on the pilot."

"Shit," Dalton muttered. "The guy must have a buttload of information if the Russians were ballsy enough to send people to spy on the meeting."

"Maybe not," Nash argued. "If it were so important, why would they grab up two women who didn't have base access to do the job?"

"I'm pretty sure they were the backup plan," Logan said. "The Navy guy we found dead at the warehouse was the Coronado NAB security manager. One of the guys from the CIA said they found a hundred thousand dollars in an overseas account with the guy's name on it. They assume he placed the monitoring device in the main conference room and was supposed to use the recording device outside the building. Either he got a conscience at the last minute or got greedy. Regardless, if the guy had done what the Russians had paid him for, they'd have had their information, and we never would have known. Until we went back to Syria for the pilot again and got our asses handed to us."

And his gut told him they *would* be going back there.

"What about those three guys we caught?" Chasen asked. "Are they saying anything?"

Logan shook his head. "Not a damn thing. Those guys know there's nothing we can do to make them talk."

Like there was a lot he and his fellow SEALs *didn't* know about the Russian pilot.

"Speaking of beautiful women with guns," Dalton said. "Is the one who took you hostage going to get into trouble?"

"No. That's never even been a consideration," Logan told him. "I made sure the cops and the feds recognized Felicia and Stef were the victims here. Felicia only did what she had to, and I was never in any danger."

Dalton gave him a sidelong glance. "If I didn't know better, I'd think you were a little protective of her."

Logan opened his mouth to say no, but then he thought about it and decided yeah, he did feel protective of Felicia and her sister.

"Maybe," he admitted. "But it's only because I have a date with Felicia on Friday night."

"You asked a woman out for a date after she and her sister were held hostage by a group of terrorists?" Chasen let out a snort. "Man, that's seriously messed up."

"It was her idea," Logan said. "She asked me to come over to her place for dinner as a way of thanking me for helping her out."

"Uh-huh," Nash said.

Logan shook his head with a laugh. "Guys, it's just dinner."

"And is she aware you're allergic to relationships?" Dalton asked.

"Look who's talking," Logan countered. "Okay, first off, I'm not *allergic to relationships*. I simply haven't found a woman I feel serious enough about to bother getting deeply involved. And second, I never said anything about this *being* a *relationship*. One more time for the cheap seats—it's just dinner."

They ragged on him for the next two miles, reminding him about how many *dinners* he'd been to the last few years. He couldn't argue too much because they were right. He'd dated more than his share of women, and none of them had ever progressed beyond casual sex. He simply wasn't looking for more.

"You know, sometimes it doesn't matter whether you're looking for a relationship or not," Chasen said as they slowed to move through the deeper sand lining this part of the route they'd taken. "If you meet the right person, it kind of happens. I wasn't looking for anything serious either, but then everything changed when I met Hayley."

Logan had to admit he had been as surprised as the rest of the guys when Chasen fell for his girlfriend, journalist Hayley Garner. But Felicia had merely invited him over to say thanks for saving her sister. That was it.

As he jogged down the beautiful white sand beach though, a part of him hoped it might turn into something more.

Chapter Five

IF IT'S JUST dinner, you don't mind if I join you guys, right?"

Felicia paused from dumping tortilla chips into a bowl to give her sister a look. Stef had stopped by to help her get ready for her date with Logan, and after approving of the dress Felicia had picked out and declaring the Mexican food she'd made for dinner perfect, her sister had perched on a stool at the island.

Stef swiped a chip and nibbled on it. "So, it isn't *just* dinner."

"I told you," Felicia said. "This is my way of saying thank you for saving both our lives."

"So you don't think he's cute." When she didn't answer, her sister grinned. "I knew it! You asked him out because you think he's hot."

Felicia sighed. Denying it would be stupid, so she didn't bother. She'd been telling Stef all week this was simply her way of paying Logan back for what he'd done. She'd been careful to avoid using the word date because every time she went out with a guy, Stef started cueing up the wedding march.

Her sister, the romantic.

But Felicia wasn't interested in running headlong into marriage. Maybe that was a funny way for a wedding planner to act, but she'd seen enough of both the good and bad of the institution of marriage to know it was better to take things slowly when it came to deciding who you were going to spend the rest of your life with. If you didn't, that bit about *till death do us part* quickly turned into *till the lawyers take all our money*.

That said, she was definitely attracted to Logan and wouldn't mind seeing him on a regular basis. She simply wasn't ready to pick out wedding invitations yet.

Felicia took the homemade salsa out of the fridge when the doorbell rang. She glanced at the clock on the microwave. Seven o'clock. Right on time. She liked punctuality in a guy.

Stef and Chewbacca, Felicia's lab-mix, trailed behind her to the entryway like two curious puppies. While Chewy patiently hung back to see who their visitor was, Felicia's sister dashed past her to peek through the peephole. Felicia nudged her aside.

"Hey!" her sister protested. "I want to see what he looks like out of uniform."

Felicia couldn't help laughing. "You are such a spaz."

She had to admit, she was curious, too.

Running her hand down the front of her dress, she opened the door. When she'd called him earlier in the week to confirm their date, she'd told him to dress casually, and Logan had taken her at her word. She had no idea cargo shorts, a T-shirt, and beach shoes could look so spectacular on a man, but the shorts showed off his tanned, muscular legs, and the T-shirt was snug enough to see the outline of all the muscles he had hidden underneath.

"Hey," she said, giving him a smile.

"I'm not too underdressed, am I?" he asked as he took in her sleeveless dress. "We did say we'd keep in casual, right?"

She laughed and motioned him inside. "We did. You're perfectly dressed for dinner."

He looked her up and down again as he entered, his eyes lingering on her legs before traveling back up her body. Felicia swore she could feel the heat she saw there warming up her bare skin.

"You look beautiful," he said.

She blushed, momentarily at a loss for words. She pushed her long, dark hair over her shoulder to cover how flustered she suddenly was. "Thanks."

Felicia didn't know how long she and Logan stood there in the entryway gazing at each other, but it must have been longer than she thought because her sister cleared her throat.

"You remember my sister Stefanie," she said.

Logan smiled. "Yeah, of course. How're you doing?"

"It'll be a while before I stop keeping Mace at the ready when I'm walking through a parking lot, but other than that, I'm doing good," Stef said. "Thanks again for what you did."

She grabbed her purse from the couch then gave Chewy a pat on the head, her dark ponytail flipping over her shoulder as she turned back around. "I'm going to leave you two lovebirds alone. Have fun!"

When was out the door before Felicia could even give her the stink-eye or tell her to be careful. "Text me to let me know you got to the dorm, okay?" she called as the door closed behind Stef.

Sighing, Felicia turned to Logan. "Ignore my sister."

Logan chuckled. "Don't worry about it. I'm glad to see she's doing okay after what happened."

Felicia smiled. "Yeah, me, too."

She'd been worried about Stef the first few days after the kidnapping, afraid her sister might have post-traumatic stress, but by Sunday she was the same bubbly twenty-year-old she'd always been. Which was astounding to Felicia. Then again, how exactly did someone behave after they'd been kidnapped and held hostage? It wasn't like there was a handbook.

Logan crouched down to give Chewy a pet. "Who's this guy?"

Felicia smiled. "This is Chewbacca, but I call him Chewy for short."

Logan flashed her a grin. "Big *Star Wars* fan, huh?"

"Huge," she admitted then added, "I know. I'm a nerd."

He chuckled as he got to his feet. "Then it makes me one, too. I've got the original movies on Blu-Ray."

"I don't feel so bad then," she said. "Can I get you a beer?"

Logan nodded. "Thanks."

He followed her over to the island separating the kitchen from the living room. "How the heck did you get a condo this close to the beach, and in Pacific Beach no less? This area is always in demand."

She glanced at him over her shoulder as she reached into the fridge to grab a beer for him and a wine cooler for her. "My parents owned it, and I kept it after they passed away. It's the only way I could ever afford to live here."

Regret crossed his face. "I had no idea your mom and dad were gone. I'm sorry."

She set the bottle of beer on the counter in front of him. "Thanks."

"How old were you and your sister when they passed away?"

"I was twenty-two and Stef was sixteen."

He shook his head. "Damn. That must have been tough."

"It was." She gave him a small smile. "But now I don't have anything except happy memories of them."

"I'm glad." He opened the bottle and took a swig of beer then looked around. "Do you need any help with dinner?"

She grinned. "I'm making you dinner, remember? Besides, everything is already in the oven."

Picking up a chip, she dipped it into the fresh salsa then popped it into her mouth. On the other side of the island, Logan did the same.

"If I didn't know better, I'd think these were homemade," he said.

"They are. I made them. The salsa, too."

"You made chips and salsa?" He regarded her in awe. "Okay, consider me impressed."

"They're actually very easy to make."

"For you, maybe. I'm the guy who can burn things in a microwave, remember?" He helped himself to another chip. "How'd you get so good at it?"

Felicia laughed. "I'm a wedding planner, and when my partner and I first started our business, we had to do all our own catering, including making wedding cakes. We both honed our skills in the kitchen really fast."

He glanced at her as he scooped up

some salsa on his chip. "How'd you end up as a wedding planner? Did you go to college, or was it an on-the-job thing?"

His question surprised her. The guys she usually dated freaked when they found out she was a wedding planner. It was like they were afraid she was sizing them up for tuxedos the moment they met.

"I have a BA in hospitality management, but learned most of what I know after I got my first job," she told him. "The biggest thing you have to be able to do is multi-task. Cooking, baking, sewing, counseling, money management—you have to do it all. My partner Heather and I have seen everything from the mothers of the bride and groom throwing cake at each other to the best man texting during the ceremony. Right now, we're helping a crazy bride who insists on having a sunrise wedding on the beach even though she never gets out of bed before noon."

Logan chuckled. "That seems fraught with problems."

"No kidding. She's driving Heather and me insane." Felicia sipped her wine cooler. "You ready to eat dinner?"

If they didn't, she'd end up helping him devour the whole bowl of tortilla chips.

"I didn't know what you'd prefer, so I made chicken, beef, and veggie burritos," she said as she carried the casserole dish over to the table. "Which would you like?"

"You pick first," he said. "I'll take

whatever's left."

Felicia did a double take. A guy who let her have first choice? She didn't think men like him existed anymore.

"I appreciate it, but it's not an either or thing." She sat down across from him. "I made several of each."

The look of wonderment was back on Logan's face. "If I'd known all I had to do to get a homemade meal like this was to save a woman from Russian kidnappers, I would have done it a long time ago."

She put both a chicken burrito and a beef one on his plate. "It would have been a lot easier if you'd seen me around town and asked me out. I would have gladly made dinner for you—no Russian kidnappers required."

He regarded her with interest. "You really would have said yes if I'd walked up to you in the grocery store and asked you out?"

Felicia almost laughed. He honestly didn't know how insanely hot he was, did he?

"I really would have said yes," she told him matter-of-factly.

Hell, as good looking as he was, she might have asked him out.

Across from her, Logan used his fork to cut into the beef burrito. "You impressed me with how you handled yourself the other day, you know."

She grimaced. "I was scared out of my mind."

He looked at her. "But you did what

you thought necessary to save your sister. That's all that matters."

Felicia blushed at the blatant admiration she saw in his eyes. "I didn't get around to asking the other day. What kind of work do you do in the Navy?"

"I'm a SEAL."

She blinked. A SEAL? *Um, wow!* Despite living in San Diego all her life, she knew jack about the Navy, but even she knew about SEALs. They were like superheroes or something. She wasn't surprised to hear Logan was one. In her mind, he was standard-issued hero material.

"Are you from San Diego originally?" she asked.

He shook his head. "North Carolina. These burritos are really good, by the way."

She cut into her chicken burrito. "You don't have much of a Southern accent."

"I used to," he admitted. "I lost most of it after I joined the Navy and traveled around."

"Did you always want to be a SEAL?"

His mouth edged up. "Not really. My father is retired Army, and figured I'd follow in his footsteps like my two older brothers did, but instead I shocked the hell out of everyone and enlisted in the Navy. I've always been a rebel. Plus, I really love the water."

Felicia cringed. "I don't know much about the military, but I can't imagine it went over too well with your dad."

Logan chuckled as he pushed away his empty plate. "Not at first. But he's okay with it, now."

As she finished eating, he made her laugh, regaling her with stories about being the only sailor in a family of soldiers.

"My dad and brothers still crow like roosters every time Army beats Navy in football," he added. "My mom usually ends up playing referee."

Even though she insisted he sit, Logan helped her clear the table after dinner. They worked surprisingly well together, not getting in each other's way even once. She and Stef couldn't even do it.

"I have cake for dessert," she said as she transferred the leftover burritos to a plastic container. "Want some?"

Logan flashed her a grin. "I never say no to dessert."

In the living room, Chewy lifted his head from the couch at the mention of dessert, but then put it back down on his paws again after figuring out he wouldn't get any of it.

When she took one small cake out of the fridge then three others—each a different flavor—his eyes widened.

"Tell me you didn't make all these cakes for me."

She laughed. "No. These are samples different caterers give my partner and me in the hope we'll hire them to make wedding cakes. Perks of the business."

They sat at the kitchen table for the next two hours tasting the different cakes and talking about everything from what kind of movies they liked to whether the Chargers would make the Super Bowl. It was refreshing to be with a guy who didn't think sports were strictly a male domain.

She'd opened her mouth to suggest they go into the living room when Logan asked if she wanted to go for a walk on the beach.

"It seems a shame to live this close to the ocean and not make use of it," he added.

Felicia couldn't remember the last time she'd been out for a romantic stroll on the sand, and she couldn't think of a better guy to do it with.

She smiled. "I'd love to."

It was a short two-block walk to the beach. When they got there, they kicked off their shoes and left them behind some rocks so they could walk across the wet sand barefoot. The moonlight reflected off the gentle surf, making the already perfect evening seem more magical, and before long, they held hands.

They were talking about which sampler cake was their favorite when Logan suddenly stopped and turned her to face him. Even in the dark, she couldn't mistake the hunger in his eyes.

He was going to kiss her.

Pulse skipping a beat, she went up on tiptoe, meeting him halfway.

When his mouth came down on hers, she moaned, loving the way the salty sea spray on his lips mixed with the hint of chocolate still left on his tongue from the cakes they'd sampled. But the delicious, masculine taste uniquely Logan's was even more powerful than either of those. She ran her hands up the front of his T-shirt, exploring the muscles beneath as she savored every little bit of him.

One hand slid into her long hair while the other glided down her back to cup her ass through the thin material of her dress and sending tingles chasing all over her body. That was when she noticed the solid and very sizable bulge in the front of his cargo shorts. Knowing he was as turned on as she was made her whimper out loud.

She'd never done anything as crazy as make out on the beach before, even one that was deserted at this time of night. But as Logan trailed kisses along her jaw and down her neck, she decided that maybe she should be open to new experiences.

Logan lifted his head and slowly spun her around until she faced the ocean, her back pressed tightly against him. His arms came around her, wrapping around her middle and tugging her closer until her ass was firmly against the hard-on in his shorts.

She let her head fall back on his muscular chest, rotating her hips ever so slightly. Logan pressed his lips to the curve of her neck with a groan, one hand cupping her breast. It would be so easy to do it right here on the beach in the dark. She could lift the back of her dress while he unzipped his shorts. They could stand like this and no one would have a clue. Until she cried out in pleasure, of course.

The idea of doing something so crazy shocked her. She liked playing it safe, especially when it came to men. But being with a man as gorgeous, sexy, and perfect as Logan made her want to do all kinds of insane stuff she'd never tried before.

She was trying to decide whether to reach back and undo his zipper herself or simply resort to begging him to take her right there on the beach when Logan leaned over and whispered in her ear.

"You're starting to shiver. We should go back to your apartment."

Felicia wanted to tell him her shivering had nothing to do with the cold breeze coming off the waves and everything to do with him, but she could only nod. Was it too much to hope he'd suggest they go somewhere more private?

But when they got to her apartment and she asked if he wanted to come in, he shook his head.

"I want to, I really do," he murmured, his voice low and sexy. "More than you could possibly imagine."

Felicia doubted it. Her imagination was working overtime right about then.

"But if I go inside with you, we're going

to pick up where we left off at the beach," he added.

"Is that so bad?" she countered.

He chuckled softly. "Not at all. But I think maybe we should take our time. Call me crazy, but I'm getting the feeling we have a spark. It might be nice to see where it goes if we let it."

The part of her that wanted to rip his clothes off on the beach was bummed, but the part that liked to take her time when it came to relationships was thrilled she might finally have found a guy who felt the same way she did about these things.

She smiled. "I'm good with that. I don't mind taking our time."

Logan kissed her long and slow, and the touch of his lips was almost enough to make her change her mind.

He pulled away to grin down at her. "One of the guys on the Team is having a promotion party and cookout on Sunday at his place. Would you'd like to go with me? If it isn't too soon to go out again, I mean."

Too soon? Heck, she was ready to go on another date right now.

"I'd love to," she said.

He leaned in for another kiss. "I'll pick you up at noon."

Felicia leaned back against the door and watched Logan walk to his SUV. Sunday couldn't come fast enough.

Chapter Six

THE COUPLE HOSTING the party—the SEAL from the warehouse named Chasen and his girlfriend Hayley—lived in a cute apartment complex about thirty minutes from Felicia's condo. She was excited to meet Logan's teammates even though she was still a little confused about how the whole promotion thing worked in the Navy.

"Explain to me again why the guy who's getting promoted has to pay for his own party," she said when Logan came around to open the passenger door for her. "It seems kind of backward."

Logan chuckled as they walked hand-in-hand down the sidewalk in front of the building. "It's a very old military tradition. The person getting promoted is expected to spend the difference between his old rank and his new rank on the party as a way of sharing his good fortune with his Teammates, typically, in the form of free food and alcohol."

Felicia shook her head, still not understanding. "It must be a guy thing."

He stopped to pull her in for a kiss. "Did I tell you that you look beautiful?"

She wore another sleeveless dress, this one in a colorful boho print. "Yes, but I don't mind if you want to tell me again." She took in his cargo shorts and dark blue T-shirt with a smile. "You look pretty darn good yourself."

Instead of heading for the entrance of the building, Logan led her around the back of the complex to the grassy common area set up with chairs, picnic tables, and grills. From the looks of all the people there, the party was already in full swing.

Logan placed the bean and cheese dip she'd made on the table with the rest of the food then introduced her to everyone. Felicia recognized Nash and Dalton from the warehouse, but there were at least a dozen more SEALs. She tried to commit all their names to memory, but after a while they got lost in the sea of buff Navy hunks. If she wasn't so stuck on Logan already, Felicia would have been in serious danger of stepping on her bottom lip and tripping herself.

"Are all these guys on SEAL Team 5?" she asked Logan.

He nodded. "Chasen, Nash, Dalton, Holden, Wes, Dean, and Kurt are the only ones in my platoon though." When she looked at him confusion, he added, "SEAL Team 5 is made up of eight smaller groups called platoons, and there are sixteen guys in each platoon."

Okay, she seriously needed a handbook to keep track of all this. She was a little surprised at how many of the guys were at the party solo, though. But besides Dalton, who was with a California surfer girl named Summer, and Kurt and his wife Melissa, none of the others seemed to have significant others.

"Chasen told me what happened with you and your sister," Hayley said when Logan introduced her. "I'm glad you two are okay."

Felicia smiled. "Thanks to Logan." She glanced at him. "If it weren't for him and the other guys, Stef and I probably wouldn't be here right now."

Hayley waved her hand. "They're paid to be heroic. I'm more impressed with you, Felicia. You seriously shoved a gun in Logan's back and took him hostage? Now, that's what I call epic."

"More like desperate," Felicia said.

"Well, I want to hear all about it," Hayley said. "Come sit down."

So she and Logan sat at one of the picnic tables with Hayley, Chasen, Kurt, and Melissa, and told the other two couples the whole story. While they all agreed with Logan and Hayley about Felicia being incredibly brave, Felicia was more awestruck with how Hayley and Chasen had met. Between the Boko Haram capturing Hayley and threatening her with execution, and a rescue in the pitch black of night, it sounded like something out of a movie.

"How did you guys meet?" Felicia asked Melissa and Kurt when Hayley and Chasen had finished.

Melissa glanced at her husband, her dark eyes dancing. "He balanced a ball on his nose to impress me."

Beside Felicia, Logan did a double take.

"Wait. What?" he said.

"How come we never heard about it?" Chasen asked, looking equally stunned.

Kurt scowled. "Because it's need-to-know, and you don't need to know."

His answer didn't stop Logan and Chasen from badgering him for more details. Finally, Kurt muttered something about a SEAL named Wes manning the grill.

"I'd better check on the kid before he burns the burgers," he said.

Logan and Chasen exchanged looks, something unspoken passing between them. A moment later, they both announced they'd be right back then followed Kurt, clearly determined to get their friend to spill the beans.

"Did Kurt really balance a ball on his nose?" Hayley asked Melissa after the guys took off.

Melissa nodded. "He came to my classroom for career day, and my first-graders insisted if he were a real seal, he could balance a ball on his nose. So he did."

Felicia laughed, trying to picture the dark-haired SEAL doing something so cute to impress his future wife.

"It took me a while to realize it, but I fell in love with him right then," Melissa added.

Felicia sipped her iced tea. "When did you and Kurt get married?"

"Nineteen ninety-four." Melissa regarded her thoughtfully. "Being with a SEAL isn't always easy, not with the kind of job they do. But if you fall in love with one, it's worth it."

Beside Felicia, Hayley nodded. "What Logan, Chasen, and the other guys did the other day in the warehouse is typical everyday stuff for a SEAL."

Felicia had thought she knew what SEALs did for a living, but she discovered her knowledge base was dreadfully inadequate. According to Hayley and Melissa, SEALs were in every craphole around the world at that moment. It didn't take a genius to figure out this was the other women's way of giving her a heads-up in case this thing between her and Logan turned into something more. She could appreciate that.

Logan, Chasen, and Kurt came back a little while later, though whether they'd gotten Kurt to talk was anyone's guess. Melissa and Kurt's fourteen-year-old daughter Madison and sixteen-year-old twin boys Kayden and Ashton showed up a few minutes later. Dark-haired like their parents, Madison had Kurt's blue eyes while Kayden's and Ashton's were brown like Melissa's.

"Did you tell everyone yet?" Madison asked her parents excitedly.

"Not yet." Melissa smiled her husband. "Do you want to do the honors?"

Kurt grinned back then looked around at the rest of them. "I'm retiring."

"No way!"

A chorus of incredulity followed that exclamation. Felicia glanced over her shoulder to see Nash, Dalton, and the other SEALs gathered around the table.

Kurt slipped his arm around Melissa, his grin broadening. "You better believe it. I already filed my paperwork. Six months then I'm going ashore."

Nash looked dumbfounded. "How are we going to function without you here to keep us straight?"

Kurt jerked his head at Chasen. "That's what he's for now. Retiring means Mack won't be forced to move Chasen to another platoon."

His words seemed to mollify all the guys, including Logan.

"So what are you going to do with yourself?" Chasen asked.

Kurt glanced at his wife. "I'm taking a contractor instructor position at BUD/s."

Logan must have realized from the look on Felicia's face she didn't know what the acronym stood for because he leaned close.

"Basic Underwater Demolition SEAL

training," he explained. "It's basically six months of hell."

That didn't sound fun at all, and yet Logan grinned as he sat back.

"Speaking of BUD/s," Nash said. "How's Sam doing?"

Logan put his mouth to Felicia's ear again. "Sam is Kurt and Melissa's son."

On the other side of the table, Melissa's dark eyes clouded with worry, but Kurt looked every inch the proud father.

"Kicking butt and taking names like I knew he would," Kurt said.

"Do you think HQ is going to put Sam on SEAL Team 5?" Dalton asked.

Kurt shook his head. "I doubt it."

"Well, I hope they do. In fact, I've been pestering Mack about it ever since Sam started training," Melissa said. "I'm not thrilled he wanted to be a SEAL since it's one more guy I'm going have to worry about now along with the rest of you, but I'd feel a lot better if he's at Coronado so I can keep an eye on him."

"Don't you mean mother him?" Madison teased with a grin.

Melissa shook her head. "Keeping an eye on him isn't mothering him."

"Yeah, it kind of is," Madison pointed out. "They call it being a hover mom."

Kurt chuckled.

Melissa ignored him. "I do not hover. I simply want to be able to warn him off women who are only interested in him because he's a SEAL."

Madison laughed. "Mom, I'm pretty sure Sam doesn't need you protecting his virtue from a bunch of frog hogs."

Felicia looked at Logan. "Frog hog?" she whispered.

"SEAL groupies," he whispered back.

There were so many women who chased after SEALs, there was a name for them? Although from looking at the guys here today, she could believe it. She didn't know why, but for some strange reason, she suddenly felt very possessive of Logan.

Across from Felicia, Melissa's eyes widened. "Where did you hear that expression, daughter?"

Madison grinned and looked pointedly at Kurt, who suddenly decided he needed to go check on Wes and the burgers—again.

Felicia laughed along with everyone else. She couldn't remember having so much fun at a party. While the guys might like to rag on each other, not to mention play damn hard to win a game of touch football for bragging rights, it was obvious SEAL Team 5 was one big family, and she couldn't help but feel a little honored to be included in it.

* * * * *

"It's called center mass, baby!" Petty Officer Trent Wagner crowed in his Texas drawl as he pointed downrange at the target he'd fired at with his HK MP5N submachine gun. "Every round in the ten circle of the chest."

Logan snorted. He and his guys were at the shooting range to get in a little target practice with another platoon from SEAL Team 5. As it always did whenever they got together, it had turned into a competition. And right now, the other seven guys from Trent's platoon hooted and hollered at shooting that looked damn hard to outdo.

Well, he'd never been the type to shy away from a challenge.

"Don't get cocky, kid," Logan said as he walked up to the line with his M4A1 assault rifle. "Let me show you how it's really done."

Trent regarded the shortened version of the tried and true M16 rifle used by the US military in one form or another since the Vietnam War, his hazel eyes full of amusement. "With that old thing? You sure you don't want to give up now and avoid the embarrassment?"

Trent's platoon broke into another round of chuckles. Logan ignored them. Trent was trying to get in his head. But it would take somebody a lot better at psychological operations than SEAL Team 5's resident cowboy to do that.

Logan leveled his gaze at Trent. "Watch and learn, Cowboy."

Taking a deep breath, he let it out then jacked the rifle up to his shoulder in one smooth, well-practiced move. A moment later, he squeezed the trigger, putting each of the thirty rounds in the M4's magazine through the man-shaped target's head. Not the fifteen-meter target Trent had been shooting at, but the twenty-five-meter target.

He flashed Trent a grin. "Now, that's center of mass, baby."

Trent shook his head with a laugh. "Nice shooting, dude."

Several hundred rounds later, Trent's platoon took off along with a good portion of Logan's to bring the weapons back, leaving him, Trent, Chasen, Nash, Dalton, and Holden to clean up the range.

"Chasen, did I read this morning's paper right about the Nesbitt case going to trial?" Dalton asked from the other side of the range as they brought in the targets. "I thought you said that asshole was going to take a plea deal?"

Chasen's girlfriend Hayley was at the center of the prosecutor's case against the dirty former city councilman William Nesbitt. If anyone knew the latest on the case, it was Chasen.

"The DA expected some type of plea by now, but Nesbitt seems content to take this to trial," Chasen said. "The DA is worried Nesbitt's got something up his sleeve, but he isn't sure what Nesbitt's angle is."

Logan frowned. "But they caught him with the damn murder weapon. We might know he didn't actually pull the trigger himself, but having a murder weapon in your possession should count for something, right?"

Chasen shrugged. "You'd think so."

"Okay, someone want to fill me in here?" Trent asked. "I mean, I heard rumors some of you guys were involved in Nesbitt getting arrested, but this sounds like you know more than the cops do."

Logan saw Chasen hesitate. Not because he didn't trust Trent, but because this crap with Nesbitt was way outside the usual mission parameters. Telling Trent essentially made him an accessory after the fact.

"Whatever you tell me, I won't say anything," Trent added as he brought in the last of the targets.

Chasen leaned back against the counter and crossed his arms over his chest. "You already know the basic stuff in the news, right? Nesbitt is a crooked politician who got caught in a complex kickback scheme revolving around the new SEAL construction project at Imperial Beach. He got paid money under the table from the prime contractor, Jack Yates, in exchange for arranging the assassination of a city inspector who was about to name Yates as the responsible party behind a highway collapse that killed some people."

"Yeah, I heard all that." Trent said. "Didn't the prime contractor turn states evidence or something on Nesbitt?"

"Uh-huh. But the DA is worried it won't be enough. No one's thrilled with taking one criminal's word over another. The real damning evidence against Nesbitt is the murder weapon the police recovered. Ballistics has ID'd it as the weapon that killed the city inspector."

Trent frowned. "I still don't see where you guys fit into this whole thing."

Chasen exchanged looks with Logan. This part could get them into hot water if anyone ever found out.

"The cops recovered the weapon used to kill the city inspector because the four of us," Chasen gestured to Logan, Nash, and Dalton, "broke into Nesbitt's house in the middle of the night because I thought the man had kidnapped Hayley—which he hadn't. Anyway, he came after us with a bunch of his private security guys. It turned into a flat-out gun battle in the most expensive neighborhood in San Diego."

Trent's eye's widened. "No shit! Does the old man know?"

"Hell, no." Chasen grimaced. "If he did, we'd all probably be in Leavenworth breaking big rocks into little rocks. The problem is, Nesbitt knows we broke in. I'm worried he's going to try to use it to get himself out of this somehow."

Logan ground his jaw. The dirtbag should already be serving a life sentence for the part he played in the city inspector's death. "How could he use it?"

Chasen's mouth tightened. "Let's say Hayley had a theoretical conversation with the DA. According to her, if Nesbitt's lawyer can make the break-in seem like some kind of extreme federal government overreach, he might be able to get the weapon tossed out as evidence. If that happens, the case will probably be tossed out as well."

Trent considered that. "Then what happens to you guys?"

"Hello Fort Leavenworth. Good-bye freedom."

"Damn," Trent muttered. "If you guys ever need help with that asshole, call me." He checked his watch. "I'm going to get out of here. See you around."

Logan and the other guys climbed into his SUV a few minutes later.

"Felicia seems nice," Chasen said conversationally from the passenger seat as Logan turned onto the road.

Logan had wondered when someone would bring Felicia up in conversation. He gave his friend a sidelong glance.

"She's very nice."

Not to mention beautiful, sexy, and captivating. She was also smart, fun to talk to, and a fantastic cook. Oh, and when she kissed him, it damn near brought him to his knees. He could only imagine how good it would be when he and Felicia finally slept together.

He sure as hell wasn't going to tell these guys any of that, though.

"And she handled the heaping serving of reality Kurt said Melissa and Hayley gave her without running for the hills," Dalton remarked. "That definitely bodes well for the future of your relationship."

Logan looked at his Teammate in the rearview mirror. "Bodes well? Who the hell talks like that? And for the tenth time, there is no relationship. I'm focused on the here and now. That's as far forward as I want to think about right now."

"Uh-huh," Dalton said. "You guys heard that, right?"

Chasen and Nash nodded.

"Yup," Nash agreed. "He said *right now*. I heard it clear as day."

"You're already starting to caveat your denials," Chasen said. "It won't be long before you're telling us you and Felicia aren't getting married...*right now*."

Logan looked over at Chasen to see him grinning from ear to ear.

"What the hell is so funny?" he asked sharply.

"Nothing," Chasen said then added, "Right now, at least."

Logan wanted to tell them Felicia wasn't any different than any other woman he'd gone out with, but he couldn't make himself say the words. Because no matter how much he tried to deny it—even to himself—Felicia was different. If not, he would have slept with her a couple of times already and moved on. Resisting the urge to take her to bed after kissing her on the beach the first night hard been difficult enough. He should probably be given a medal for refusing to give in to his more primal instincts after making out on her couch when they'd come back from the cookout yesterday. The mere thought of how she'd straddled his lap and wiggled while they'd kissed was enough to make him hard in his uniform pants.

But just because he wanted to take things slowly with Felicia didn't mean he planned on getting himself fitted for a tux. It simply meant she was more special to him than the other women he'd gone out with. There really wasn't anything more monumental about it.

At least for right now.

Chapter Seven

FELICIA AND HER sister hadn't had a girls' night out since before the kidnapping, so as far as she was concerned, they were long overdue. Other than a few quick phone calls and some texts, they hadn't even talked much since Stef had come over to help her get ready for her date with Logan, and neither of them had said anything about what had happened in the warehouse. Felicia wanted to make sure she was okay.

Since it was a Tuesday night and Stef had an early class the next morning, Felicia suggested takeout from one of their favorite Lebanese restaurants. Stef offered to pick something up on the way over and showed up promptly at six-thirty with two servings of chicken tawook. Chewy gave the marinated chicken a longing look before going back to his bowl of dog food.

Felicia speared a piece of chicken, savoring the tangy combination of yogurt, lemon, and garlic coating it. "So how have you been doing?"

Stef glanced up from her plate. "Good."

Felicia gave her a look. "I mean how are you really doing?"

"I'm fine," Stef said.

"Stef, you got kidnapped. I'm pretty sure you're the opposite of fine."

On the other side of the table, Stef frowned. "You got kidnapped, too." She sighed. "Look, I know you worry about me, but I'm okay. Really."

Felicia searched her face, looking for something to indicate her sister was dealing with stuff and not telling her. But she didn't see anything to make her doubt Stef. Then why did she get the feeling her sister was hiding something?

"Enough about me," Stef said. "I want to hear about you and Logan."

It was an obvious attempt to change the subject, but Felicia let it slide.

"What do you want to know?" she asked.

Stef sipped her iced tea. "How your date went the other night, for starters."

Felicia's lips curved. "It went great. I don't think I've ever had so much fun hanging out with a guy before. We even went for a moonlight stroll on the beach."

Her sister's eyes lit up. "Oooh, sounds romantic."

"It was."

Stef scooped up some chicken with her

fork. "Did you kiss?"

Felicia laughed. "Yes, Nosy Nellie."

"And did he spend the night?"

"No!" But she'd wanted him to. "Stef, it was our first date."

"So? Do you have a three-date rule before sleeping with a guy or something?"

More like a five-date rule, but she didn't tell her sister that. "Logan and I both want to take things slowly, that's all."

Stef grinned. "Sound like you guys are getting serious already."

Felicia reached for her iced tea. "It was just one date, Stef. Well, two counting the cookout we went to on Sunday. Even so, it's way too early to be talking about getting serious with a guy."

Her sister scowled. "That's crap. When you find the right guy, you know it."

It was Felicia's turn to frown. "That sounds like something out of a romance book. Stef, love is more than lust and attraction. It's about getting to know each other over time and making sure you're compatible with each other. It's about having the same goals and plans, and having a true long-term commitment to each other."

Stef snorted. Picking up her empty plate, she carried it over to the dishwasher. "That's not a relationship. That's a business deal."

"That's being smart." Felicia followed her sister over to the dishwasher, plate in hand. "Heck, Mom and Dad dated for five years before they got married."

Her sister shook her head. "That's insane." She glanced at her watch. "I have to get going."

"Already?"

Stef nodded. "Craig has class tonight, and I want to see him before he leaves."

Craig Bowers was Stef's boyfriend.

"Okay. Drive carefully. And text me when you get home," Felicia said.

"I will." Stef gave Chewy's ear a playful tug. "You're a guy. Talk some sense into my sister about Logan, would you?"

Felicia rolled her eyes. Her sister was way too idealistic for her own good. Stef was also very good about changing the subject. They hadn't even talked about how she was dealing with getting kidnapped. Then again, maybe not talking about it *was* how Stef dealt with it.

Sighing, Felicia finished cleaning up then turned on the TV and curled up on the couch with her laptop to surf the Web. But while she caught up on her email and fooled around on Pinterest for a little bit, she spent more time thinking about Logan.

She hadn't wanted to admit it to Stef, but she was cautiously eager to see where this thing with him went next. To bed was the obvious place, and while she was all for that, she meant beyond that. Despite what she'd said to Stef about it being too early to get serious with him, there was definitely potential for a long-term relationship.

Two hours and nearly a hundred Repins on Pinterest later, Felicia got ready for bed then snuggled under the blankets with the most recent fabric swatches she and Heather were mulling over for the upcoming weddings they' be doing in the fall.

Once again, thoughts of Logan intruded, only this time, she got distracted by his amazing kisses. She was just thinking about which parts of her anatomy she'd like him to put that talented mouth of his on when her cell phone rang.

She grabbed it off the nightstand, expecting to see Stef's name on the screen, but instead it was Logan. Had his ears been burning?

Pulse skipping a beat, she thumbed the green button and put the phone to her ear. "Hey!"

"Hey yourself." His deep, sexy voice washed over her. "I didn't wake you, did I?"

"No. I'm just lying in bed looking at color swatches."

And fantasizing about you.

"Lying in bed, huh?" he said. "What are you wearing?"

"A tank top and a pair of panties."

"That's quite the image. Wish I were there," he said then added, "Although if I were, you probably wouldn't be wearing the bra and panties for long."

Mmm, she liked the sound of that. If she closed her eyes, she could almost feel his hands on her bare skin. "Oh? And what would you do after you took them off?"

"For starters, I'd explore every inch of your naked body with my mouth, starting at the sensitive little spot behind your ear and working my way down."

Heat coalesced between her legs, making her catch her breath. "Sounds like it could take a while. Not that I'm complaining. Although," she added, "I'm having a little trouble picturing exactly what you'd be doing. Maybe you should describe it to me in detail."

Logan chuckled softly then did exactly that.

* * * * *

Logan couldn't help grinning as he walked into Wedded Bliss the following day. The chief had told him to take the rest of the afternoon off as a way of making up for all the extra crap he'd taking from Commander Hunt lately, so he'd made a beeline for Felicia's office to see if she could get away for lunch. With huge framed photos of models in beautiful bridal gowns on the walls, colorful flower arrangements positioned here and there, and granite counters covered with fancy parchment invitations, not to mention a bookcase full of bridal magazines, the place was a bride's dream house.

Felicia sat at her desk near the back wall, surrounded by stacks of bridal magazines, and she looked up at his entrance. "Hey! I didn't know you were going to stop by."

He returned her smile. "I got the rest

of the day off and thought I'd stop in and take you out to lunch."

Grin broadening, Felicia stood and came out from behind the desk to give him a kiss. "I'd love to go."

She gazed up at him for a moment, the twinkle in her eyes making him wonder if she was thinking about last night's telephone conversation.

On the other side of the room, someone cleared their throat.

Felicia's eyes widened. She turned and gestured to the blond woman seated at the other desk. "Oh! Logan, this is my friend and business partner, Heather Morris. Heather, meet Logan Dunn."

Heather came around the desk to shake his hand. Petite and curvy, she was all smiles and Southern charm. "It's a pleasure to finally meet you. Felicia has told me so much about you I feel like we're friends already."

"Felicia's told me a lot about you, too." He looked at Felicia. "You ready to go?"

"Yup. Let me grab my purse."

"Actually, since Logan has off, why don't you go ahead and take the rest of the day?" Heather suggested to Felicia.

"I can't," Felicia protested. "I have a ton of work."

"And it will all still be here tomorrow, so go!" Heather made a shooing motion toward the door. "It's too beautiful a day for both of us to stay cooped up in the office. Go hit the beach or something, sugar."

Felicia gave him a questioning look. "What do you think?"

He grinned. Did she even need to ask? "I think it sounds like a plan."

"See?" Heather said.

Felicia laughed. "Okay, okay! We'll go. But you have to promise to take a day for yourself next week."

Heather nodded. "Sure thing, sugar. And if you find a blond-haired, blue-eyed surfer hunk looking for a little southern hospitality, send him my way."

"She's like a force of nature," Logan said with a chuckle as he and Felicia walked outside.

Felicia laughed. "Yes, she is. It's part of why I love her."

"How'd the two of you become business partners?"

"We worked together at the event planning company I mentioned to you the other night. We both wanted to focus on weddings so we decided to open our own business."

He came to a stop beside her SUV. "I need to stop by my place to change. Meet you at your condo in thirty minutes?"

"If you want to bring some clothes for after the beach, you can shower up at my place then we can go out to dinner," she suggested. "There's this new place in Mission Valley I've been wanting to try. They cater receptions, and I'd like to see what their menu is like."

Even if she was combining business and pleasure, it still sounded good to Logan. He couldn't think of anything better than hitting the beach with a beautiful woman on a hot, sunny day followed by good food someone else made.

He bent his head to kiss her. "See you in half an hour."

Luckily traffic wasn't too insane so he made it to his apartment in record time. Ditching his uniform, he changed into swim trunks and a T-shirt then stuffed jeans and a button-down in a weekender.

By the time he got to Felicia's condo, she'd changed out of the long skirt and blouse she'd had on into a pair of cut-off shorts and a tank top. Logan had been hoping for something skimpy and/or see-through, so he was a little bummed by her choice of clothing. Not that she didn't look spectacular. The cutoffs showed plenty of sexy leg, and her top was thin enough to hint at the curves underneath. He kept his disappointment in check, figuring she'd strip down a little more when they actually hit the sand.

His patience was rewarded. After getting to the same beach where they'd gone for a moonlit stroll the other night and they had spread out their towels, Logan had the immense pleasure of watching Felicia strip off her tank top to expose a red bikini top working overtime to contain some amazing curves. Then, just when he thought it couldn't get any better, she undid the snap on her cut-off jeans and started to do that shimmy thing all women were somehow genetically gifted with. His damn jaw nearly thumped onto the sand as she shoved her shorts over her hips and granted him a vision of the tiny bikini bottoms designed to match the top and melt his soul at the same time.

Oh God, he was in heaven. Felicia wasn't simply hot. She was frigging incendiary!

Thankfully, she didn't notice him staring. Okay, maybe she did. It was kind of hard to miss. But at least she didn't call him on it. She simply took her time putting her shorts and top in her tote bag, letting him having his fun.

After she finished, she turned back to him with a smile. "Mind putting this on for me?" she asked, handing him a bottle of sunscreen.

He grinned. "My pleasure."

Logan tried to be good and keep his hands to the appropriate places, but if they wandered down to rub lotion on those parts of her ass cheeks left exposed by her suit, it was only because he wanted to make sure she was adequately protected from the sun.

That was his story, and he was sticking to it.

Felicia didn't seem to mind, if the amount of amount of time she spent massaging lotion into his back and shoulders was any indication. He couldn't help noticing she let her hands slip down to get those few spots he'd missed along his abs. Yeah, right. She was so busted.

By the time they lay back on their respective towels, Logan was already overheated, and it had nothing to do with the sun. Seeing Felicia lying there on a towel beside him, her sexy body glistening in the sun, was enough to get him going all by itself. It was damn tough not letting his mind wander to other places. Within moments, he was sporting a nice hard-on in his trunks. He was relatively sure Felicia noticed, but once again, she didn't seem to mind. If anything, she was blatantly ogling him—and she wasn't apologizing for it.

He reached for one of the bottles of water they'd brought with them and took a swig. "So what's going on with the sunrise wedding?"

Felicia leaned back on her elbows with a groan. "The bride is driving us crazy. Now she wants to have the reception on the beach as well as the ceremony. Oh, and she wants mimosas served before and after the ceremony—at six o'clock in the morning."

Logan chuckled. "Seriously?"

"Uh-huh. We're still trying to figure out if it's legal to serve alcohol so early in the morning in San Diego." She sighed. "The bride isn't interested in hearing that. She wants Heather and me to make it happen."

"Is she your typical bride?" he asked.

"Not really." Felicia admitted. "Most of

them aren't nearly this high-maintenance. But I'd rather put up with a hundred bridezillas like her than try to figure out what's going on with my sister at the moment."

He frowned. "What's up with Stef?"

"I'm worried she's more upset about the kidnapping than she's letting on, but when I ask her about it, she won't talk to me."

"Are you worried she might have PTSD?" he asked.

He'd seen more than his fair share of military personnel have to deal with the trauma that came from being in life and death situations. Being held hostage like Stef had been could shake anyone.

"Maybe." Felicia sighed. "I wish I could get her to talk to me about it."

"She might not be able to talk to you about it. Not because she doesn't feel she can confide in you, but because sometimes it's easier to talk to someone who isn't as close to the situation as you are." Logan regarded her thoughtfully. "What about you?"

"What about me?"

He ran a finger down her arm. "You got kidnapped, too."

She considered that. "I won't deny it freaked me out. And sometimes, I find myself thinking about it when my mind starts wandering. I'm more aware of who's around me when I walk to my car now, that's for sure. But I'm okay."

That was good to know. It still didn't stop him from wanting to kill that asshole Illarion Volkov for what he did to Felicia and her sister.

Logan leaned in and kissed her gently. "If you need someone to talk to, I'm here, okay?"

Felicia nodded. "Thanks."

"You feel like checking out that restaurant now?" he asked.

She smiled. "Sounds good."

Despite covering up all that magnificent skin, Logan had to admit watching Felicia get dressed was almost as sexy as watching her undress. Almost, but not quite, he thought as they walked back to her condo.

As she headed toward her bedroom, her beautiful ass swaying back and forth, Logan almost groaned.

"You need help getting all that sunscreen off?" he asked, trying to sound casual.

Felicia stopped mid-step and threw a heated glance over her shoulder. "I could use a hand, if you're offering."

He grinned. "I'm all about being helpful."

Chapter Eight

LOGAN SUSPECTED FELICIA'S bedroom was as beautiful as the rest of the house, but he was too busy following her into the adjoining bathroom to pay much attention to the décor.

Felicia turned on the water then gave him a repeat performance of the sexy strip show she'd put on for him at the beach, slowly taking off her top and wiggling out of her cutoffs. She probably would have done the same with her bikini, but Logan got there first.

Untying the strings holding up her top, he let it fall to the floor. Her breasts were just as perfect as he imagined and he ran his fingers over their silky softness before hooking his thumbs in her bikini bottoms and slowly pushing them over her hips and down her legs.

"Damn, you're beautiful," he breathed.

"Thank you," she said softly. "And you are wearing too many clothes."

Giving him a sultry smile, she pulled his T-shirt over his head then shoved down his swim trunks. When she finished, she stepped back and took in his naked body, starting at his chest then moving down his abs until she got to his hard cock.

"Water's getting cold," he said.

Taking her hand, he led her into the walk-in shower then closed the door behind them. Grabbing the shower gel from the rack, he squeezed some into his hand then lathered it up.

"Turn around," he said.

When she complied, he gently ran his soapy hands over shoulders and down her back, massaging her muscles while he washed away the sunscreen. Felicia scooted closer until his hard cock nestled in the crack of her delightful ass. He glided his hands down, cupping her cheeks and giving them a squeeze.

Logan wanted to linger there and let his fingers explore a little, but he controlled himself. He had more skin to clean.

So he moved his hands over her hips and around to her taut stomach. The muscles there tensed under his fingers.

"Are you ticklish?" he murmured in her ear.

She shook her head, grinding her ass against his hard-on.

Groaning, he ran his hands up her midriff to cup her breasts. She sighed, practically melting into him as he tweaked her nipples. She did a little circular dance with her ass now, and he was damn close to going nuts. It felt like he'd been hard for hours. Man, he couldn't wait to slide inside her.

He slipped one hand down, letting it settle between her legs and find its way between her folds.

Has anyone ever mentioned you have very talented fingers?" she asked.

Logan nuzzled the curve of her neck, loving the flavor of her freshly washed skin. "No. Can't really remember that ever coming up in conversation." He let one finger slide up to the top of her opening, finding her plump clit and making teasing little circles around it. "So, are you saying you like when I do this?"

"Mmm, I definitely like," she confirmed. "But go slowly. I like to be teased."

He was a good SEAL. He knew exactly when to follow orders. And in this case, he had no problem teasing her as long as she wanted.

With that in mind, he worked her clit until she quivered in his arms. Then he backed off, focusing on another part of her anatomy—her nipples, her sensitive neck, or her inner thighs. When her body relaxed, he returned to her clit, pushing her closer and closer to orgasm each time. In between, he whispered exactly how beautiful she was and how sexy she sounded when she moaned.

But the teasing stopped the moment she arched back and came—hard.

Logan wrapped one arm around her

waist, tugging her back more firmly against him as she cried out. Damn, he'd never heard such a sexy sound in his life.

Afterward, he gave her a second to catch her breath then he began moving his fingers up and down the folds of her wet pussy. As soon as she was ready, Logan intended to go back to her clit and make her come again. Because he liked hearing her moan.

But Felicia extricated herself from his arms and turned around to reach for the shower gel. "I think it's time to get you cleaned up, too."

Grinning, she squirted the liquid all over his chest. As her hands came up to lather him up, Logan decided he'd never had so much fun taking a shower in his life.

* * * * *

Felicia marveled at Logan's chest. She'd been dying to get her hands on those pecs ever since he'd taken his shirt off at the beach. Lying so close to him on the sand had gotten her aroused as heck. She'd been wet the whole time, and it had nothing to do with swimming in the ocean. She'd almost slipping a hand down between her legs to give her clit some relief more than once that afternoon. She'd controlled the urge as best she could, but she was pretty sure Logan had caught her adjusting on the towel and squeezing her thighs together a little more than necessary and known exactly what she'd been doing.

By the time they'd gotten back to her

place, she'd been ready to tackle her sexy SEAL and have her way with him right there on the floor of the living room, so when he'd suggested showering together, she'd pounced on the offer. A woman would have to be insane to turn him down.

When his clothes had come off, she'd stood there mesmerized by the pure perfection of his body. There wasn't an inch on him not honed, toned, and oh-my-God-ET-phone-home gorgeous. She couldn't imagine how much hard work it took to keep a body like his so fit.

But while he might look hot naked, there was more to Logan than his charming good looks and sexy body. The man also knew how to play her body like an instrument, and his strong hands had made her tremble like a leaf. When he'd touched her clit, she couldn't have come any faster if she'd been pleasuring herself. She'd never climaxed so hard.

Felicia took her time lathering him up, letting her hands explore every inch of him, except one. Only when she finished did she wrap her hands around his thick shaft and caress him up and down until he was so hard he throbbed. Then she dropped to her knees in front of him and took him in her mouth. Mmm, he tasted delicious.

She bobbed up and down on him fast, taking him deep. From his groans, he clearly enjoyed what she was doing. That only made her work harder. She was definitely going to make him come in her mouth. It would only be fair, right? But Logan obviously had other ideas because he reached over and turned off the water then scooped her up into his arms and carried her into the bedroom.

He tossed her gently onto the bed, making her giggle. But her laugh quickly turned into a gasp when he leaned over and slowly licked the water droplets off her body. By the time he reached her pussy, she was breathing like she'd run a marathon. She'd ever run one, but the analogy seemed right.

But no matter how much she squirmed, Logan's big hands held her thighs spread wide as he teased her folds with his tongue.

"There are condoms in the nightstand," she said hoarsely when he finally leaned back to regard her with a scorching hot look. "I don't know exactly where they are, but they're in there. Dump the whole drawer out if you have, too."

Fortunately, he didn't have to do anything so drastic. He dug the condom packet out of her nightstand faster than she would have thought possible and put it on then dragged her to the edge of the bed. A moment later, her bottom was on the edge of the mattress and her legs her up in the air. She didn't know how he knew this was one of favorite positions. She lifted her head enough to watch him line up his cock with the opening of her pussy and slide in deep.

Felicia moaned, clutching the sheets as he filled her.

Logan leaned forward, giving her a searing kiss as he began to pump his hips. She wrapped her legs around his hips to pull him in even deeper. He thrust slowly a few times, toying with her. Then, when she was completely ready, he gradually picked up the pace until he pounded into her hard enough to make her butt bounce off the bed.

She hugged him tightly even as he slipped his arms around her to hold her close. As he buried his face in her neck, she felt the familiar tingling sensation that always came before an orgasm. No way could she be ready to come again, not this fast. But the pleasure kept building, and soon she was screaming as she exploded under him.

Felicia was still recovering from her climax when Logan rolled her over and she found herself sitting astride his hips, his cock still rock hard inside her. That's when she figured out he hadn't come yet.

She collapsed on his chest, resting her hands on either side of his head. Then she rode him nice and slowly gazing into his eyes.

"Do you have any idea how beautiful you look right now?" Logan asked softly as he grabbed her hips and helped her move.

She smiled down at him. "No, but by all means feel free to tell me. I never pass on a compliment."

He chuckled, the sound husky. "Well, you're gorgeous. And if I have my way, I intend to tell you frequently."

She opened her mouth to tell him that

was perfectly fine with her when Logan's big hands came up and grabbed her bottom. She'd suspected he was an ass man when he'd been paying so much attention to it in the shower. Obviously, she'd been right.

Getting a firm grip on her butt, he rocked her up and down on his cock. Felicia whimpered and traced her lips along his jaw then down his neck and over his shoulder, alternating warm kisses and little nibbles. He tasted so good, she could eat him up.

Beneath her, his body tensed, and she knew he was about to come. But she could also sense him holding back like he was waiting for her to come again first. She adored him for that, but she'd already come twice, and she wasn't sure she could climax again for a while. And after his making her come twice already, she wanted to give him as much pleasure as he'd given her.

Leaning in close, she put her mouth to his ear and breathed out her desire in a soft whisper. "Come for me."

Her entreaty seemed to have flipped a switch. One moment Logan was thrusting hard and the next he tightened his grip on her ass and pounded up into her. Felicia closed her eyes and held on for dear life.

She hadn't thought she could come again, but she'd been wrong.

It wasn't as hard as the first two times, but it was even more special, because this time he came with her, his body clenching under hers and a deep growl of pleasure tearing from his throat.

Okay, that was simply amazing.

She lay atop him, tremors still working their way through her body and her breath coming hard and fast, beads of moisture rolling off her skin. She thought for a moment she was still wet from the shower but then realized she'd actually worked up a sweat. That had definitely never happened to her during sex before.

Felicia slid off his chest to snuggle beside him, her thigh resting possessively across his. "I think we missed our dinner reservations."

He chuckled. "I hope you have something in the house we can snack on because I don't think we're done."

That's when she felt his cock hardening under her thigh. She reached down and wrapped her hand around his shaft, marveling at how fast he could recover.

"In that case. I'm going to have my snack now," she said softly.

Then she slowly began kissing her way down his body.

Chapter Nine

LEAVING FELICIA AT o'-dark-thirty the next morning so Logan could go back to his place and change into his uniform had been hard as hell. To say last night had been amazing simply didn't do it justice. He and Felicia had make love for hours until they were both exhausted then they'd fallen asleep in each other's arms. They'd never gotten around to getting something to eat, but Logan had been more than satisfied.

He had a hard time putting what they'd done last night into coherent words, or even thoughts. Special didn't come close to describing it, and any other term would have come off sounding like a romance book cliché.

Bottom line—he was hooked.

Logan was smiling at the realization when his phone rang. He dug his cell out of his pocket, assuming it was Felicia checking to see if he'd gotten home okay. She'd wanted him to call when he got there, but maybe she'd gotten impatient and called him first. His grin broadened. Having someone to worry about him was kind of nice.

But when he saw the name in his phone, he cursed. It was headquarters.

"Dunn."

The call was short and to the point. He and his Team were going wheels up— immediately. No details on where, but then again, there never were.

Logan did a U-turn and headed for base. Everything he needed was already there, including fresh uniforms. He thumbed his contacts list, finding Felicia's number.

"You're home already?" she asked the moment she picked up. "You didn't speed, did you?"

His mouth curved. "No, I wasn't speeding. I got a call from HQ. I have to leave on a mission."

On the other end of the line, Felicia was silent for a moment. Logan braced himself, not sure what he expected exactly. But when she spoke, her voice was surprisingly calm.

"Do you know where you're going? Or how long you'll be gone?"

"No."

Logan didn't bother to add that even if knew either of those things, he couldn't tell her. He held his breath, waiting to see what she would say. He remembered Kurt telling him about the first time he'd told Melissa about a no-notice mission. It hadn't gone so well.

"Be careful," she said. "And call me when you can, okay?"

"I will," he promised. "By the way, last night was incredible."

"Yeah," she said, and he liked to think she was smiling. "It was, wasn't it?"

"I'll call you when I get back."

Logan hung up and shoved his phone in his pocket as he steered his SUV onto the bridge leading to Coronado. She'd certainly handled it better than he'd thought she would.

His hand tightened on the wheel as a bizarre thought suddenly hit him. What if the reason she'd been so cool with him going was because she didn't care one way or the other?

Okay, where the hell had that come from? Felicia had given him absolutely no reason to think that.

But, still. How many guys did he know who'd left on a mission thinking they had a girlfriend waiting for them only to return home and discover their girlfriends had moved on in his absence?

As he flashed his ID card at the MP on guard and drove onto base, he told himself it was stupid to think it would be like that with Felicia.

He only hoped it wasn't wishful thinking on his part.

* * * * *

Felicia yawned for what must be the fifth time since walking into work the following Monday morning. Not surprising.

She hadn't slept well at all since Logan had left.

She'd gotten a few hours' sleep after Logan had called and told her he was leaving on a mission the morning after they'd slept together. She'd been worried but told herself that was silly. She'd seen him and his Teammates in action. She knew how good they were at their job. He'd be fine.

She'd done okay at work Thursday, thinking about him but not allowing herself to worry. Thursday night had been okay, too, even though she'd woken up a few times, not really sure why, but merely feeling uptight.

Friday, on the other hand, sucked. She didn't remember most of what she'd done that day, since it was mostly a blur. She'd gone through the motions of working but hadn't accomplished anything.

The weekend had been even worse. She'd laid in bed both nights, Chewy at her feet, and spent more time staring at the ceiling thinking about Logan than sleeping.

Felicia was shocked by how Logan's absence affected her. Yes, she liked him, and yes, they'd slept together, and yes, it had been amazing. But she and Logan had only been dating for a short time. His being gone shouldn't be such a big deal.

But it was.

Truth be told, she was frigging worried about him. Not knowing where he was, what he was doing, and when he might come back was driving her nuts. She normally wasn't so clingy about stuff like this, but all she could think about was him.

With the sunrise wedding coming up that weekend, it shouldn't have been difficult to distract herself. She still had a buttload of last minute things to do, like confirm the caterer, the bartender, and the waitstaff, as well the people setting up the tent, tables, and chairs then cleaning everything up afterward. Despite all that, she still couldn't seem to get her act together. Every time she started a task, she found thoughts of Logan creeping in.

Felicia was reading over the new reception menu her sunrise bridezilla had emailed her this morning, realizing she'd already read the damn thing three times and couldn't remember a stupid thing on it when the door open and Hayley walked in, a dark-haired girl about Stef's age at her side.

Surprised to see Hayley, but glad for any excuse to stop staring at the ridiculous menu, Felicia stood up and stepped around her desk.

"Hey! What are you doing here?"

"I thought I'd stop by to see how you're doing," Hayley said. "I hadn't realized Logan had gone out on this mission with Chasen until Melissa told me this morning. I remember the first time Chasen left and thought you might need someone to talk to."

Over by the counter where various invitations were displayed, Heather's eyes widened. "Is that why you've been such a zombie the last few days? Why didn't you tell me Logan was gone?"

"I didn't want to make a big deal out of it," Felicia told her then hurriedly introduced Hayley before Heather could chastise her any more.

Hayley introduced the girl with her as Kyla Wells. "I thought maybe we could grab lunch while we're here?" she added.

Felicia opened her mouth to say she had too much to do, but Heather overruled her.

"Might as well have lunch. You're not getting anything done anyway."

They settled on a grill and bar three blocks from the office and within easy walking distance. After they got a table and ordered, Hayley told the story of how she and Chasen had met for Heather's benefit.

Felicia sat there wide-eyed as Hayley elaborated, confiding in them about coping with PTSD after getting held hostage in Nigeria, the crazy stuff with Nesbitt and the councilman's involvement in the death of Kyla's father, and finally the way her best friend had kidnapped and nearly killed her and himself.

"Okay, back up," Heather said, brow furrowing. "There are about a dozen parts of that story requiring more details. Like why you still go visit this Brad guy in a mental institution after he tried to kill you?"

Hayley picked up her glass of iced tea. "He's my friend, and in a lot of ways, I blame myself for what happened to him. He lost part of himself when I got kidnapped in Nigeria and he never really recovered. I go to see him a couple of times a week so he knows I'll never abandon him."

Felicia couldn't help but be impressed. She wasn't sure she could be so understanding—or forgiving.

"Is he getting better?" Heather asked tentatively.

Hayley's smile was a little sad. "Some days, like when he remembers who I am and what he did. He's ashamed and embarrassed on those days, and when he's like that, I can almost believe there's a light at the end of the tunnel."

The waiter brought their food then, interrupting the conversation, and after he left, they talked about Kyla's mission to find the man who shot her father, a hired killer named Nestor Stavros.

"I want Nesbitt to go to jail," Kyla said as she dumped ketchup on her plate. "But I'm not going to stop looking for the man who actually pulled the trigger until he's in prison, too."

Felicia dug into the grilled chicken she'd ordered. "That's going to be hard to do on your own, isn't it?"

"I'm helping her," Hayley said. "The bigger problem will be convincing the cops to arrest the murdering son of a bitch after we find him."

Felicia wanted to offer help if they

needed it, but she didn't have much experience with tracking down bad guys, much less what to do if they found him.

As they finished lunch, the conversation turned to Logan and where he and his Team might be.

"Chasen can never tell me where he's going, but if you watch the news, you can probably figure it out," Hayley said. "My guess is somewhere in West Africa, Afghanistan, or Syria. Those are the hotspots right now."

Felicia frowned. "Doesn't not knowing where Chasen is drive you crazy?"

"I'd be lying if I said it didn't," Hayley admitted. "But this is part of what I signed up for when I decided to be with a SEAL."

Felicia stared into her glass of iced tea. "I didn't intend to get emotionally involved with Logan. I invited him over for dinner because I wanted to thank him for what he did for Stef and me, and because I thought it would be fun. But before I knew it, he'd gotten under my skin."

"Let me guess," Hayley said. "You didn't realize it until he left, right? That's kind of how it seems to work."

Felicia sighed. She wasn't saying she loved Logan, but she couldn't deny she definitely had a place in her heart for the sexy Navy SEAL who'd saved her life.

Beside her, Heather shook her head. "I think you two are crazy. I couldn't date a guy who wasn't around, especially a SEAL who's deployed to dangerous places all the time. I need a man who's going to be there for me when I need him, which would be frequently."

"It's all about the math I guess," Hayley said with a smile. "For me, at least, the good outweighs the bad."

The waiter interrupted them again, this time to bring the check. Hayley and Heather immediately started squabbling over the bill, each insisting on paying. While they did, Felicia thought about the conversation they'd had.

Did she truly want to get involved with a guy who'd be gone all the time? Hell, who was she kidding? She was already involved. Which begged the question, could she accept it and deal with it the way Hayley seemed to be able to? She wasn't so sure she could, or even if she wanted to.

But the alternative meant walking away from Logan now before she could even find out what they might have. Like she'd told her sister the other night, a long-term commitment for her meant building a partnership with a guy and working toward the same life goals. In other words, planning for a future together.

Did she want to commit to a man who was probably in the middle of some crappy part of the world getting shot at right now?

The emotional part of her wanted to say, *Hell yeah!*

However, the rational part urged her to proceed with caution. *Move too fast and you might make a mistake you'll regret.*

Yet, if she moved too slowly, she might regret it anyway.

Chapter Ten

I THINK I remember this rock," Nash muttered as he moved alongside Logan through the mountainous terrain in complete darkness.

Several yards away, Dalton laughed. "I doubt it. We're miles away from where were the last time. We've just spent so much damn time over here, it's starting to feel like home."

"Yeah, well, I vote we wrap up this mission and get the hell back to San Diego before I forget what our real home looks like," Nash grumbled.

That worked for Logan The only thing that sucked worse than being back over here again so soon was being over here to do the job they should have finished two weeks ago,

He, Nash, and Dalton, along with Chasen and the CIA SOG team were once again in northern Syria, this time ten miles east of Aleppo, hoping to meet up with the local Kurdish fighters and make the exchange for the damn Russian pilot.

They'd been lucky this time, though. For one thing, the only foreign fighters they had with them were two Kurds to lead them to the place where the exchange would happen. For another, there was a major battle going on to the south of Aleppo as Syrian rebels and fighters from the al-Nusra Front mounted a major offensive against Assad's government forces there. That meant this particular part of the country was almost peaceful. The best you could hope for around here was that the people trying to kill each other did it far away from you. If he and his Team were lucky, they'd be able to pick up the pilot and get out of here without anyone ever firing a shot at them.

When they reached the coordinates for the exchange point a few miles later, they spread out and settled in to wait. They didn't know exactly when the exchange was going to go down, but something told Logan this could take a while.

"You've been kind of quiet since we got here," Chasen said softly from beside Logan as they leaned back against a huge rock formation.

Logan glanced around, taking in his surroundings through his NVGs. Nash and Dalton had moved ahead with the Kurdish guides, and Joe and his SOG team were spread out all around them. He and Chasen were relatively alone.

"Just got a lot on my mind, that's all," he said softly.

"Is it about Felicia?"

Logan's first instinct was to deny it. This wasn't the time or the place to be talking about this kind of stuff. No doubt that's why Chasen brought it up. He didn't want Logan distracted out here.

"I'm a little worried Felicia might not be able to handle the job," he admitted quietly. "Hell, I'm not sure she's going to be there when we get back."

"Did you guys have a fight before we left?" Chasen asked.

"No. She actually seemed okay with me taking off. Which concerns me even more than if we'd fought."

It was still early in their relationship—crap, he was even using that word now—but he liked her a lot more than any other woman he'd ever been with. The idea Felicia might not be there when he got back gave him a weird feeling in his chest. He hadn't felt anything like it before, and he didn't like it.

"Look," Chasen said. "It's not like I have an ass-load of experience with this kind of thing, but if you expect Felicia to be there when you get back, you need to have an honest conversation with her about how you feel."

Logan cringed "That's going to be damn hard since I'm not sure how I feel."

Chasen grunted. "You'd better figure it out because she's not going to be able to read your mind. If you don't give her a reason to stay, she won't."

The sound of approaching boots in the darkness silenced them.

"Sit tight and keep an eye on things back here." Chasen got to his feet. "I'm not sure how much I trust Joe's people and I don't want anyone slipping up behind us during the exchange."

Chasen disappeared into the darkness, leaving Logan alone to worry about their six—and think about what he'd say to Felicia when he got back.

* * * * *

The exchange went better than Logan expected. Probably because Joe walked up with a big bag full of Turkish lira and tossed it on the ground in front of the Kurdish fighters. That had effectively ended the negotiations.

The pilot was younger than Logan expected, maybe twenty-eight or twenty-nine. He looked like he'd had a rough few weeks, too. His short dark hair stuck up in places, his dark eyes were bloodshot from too little sleep, and his flight suit was scuffed and torn. When he saw Logan and his Team, his whole demeanor changed. A spark that hadn't been in his eyes before flared up now.

"He's your responsibility until we get him out of the country," Chasen said to Logan as the Kurds took their money and hightailed it out of there. "Stick to him like glue."

Joe and Chasen turned and led the way west toward the helicopters waiting for them across the border in Turkey. From there, they'd fly straight to Incirlik Air Base then hop a C5 for home. If they didn't run into any problems, they'd be back in the US in a day or so.

Logan and Nikolay stayed in the middle of the group, with Nash and Dalton taking the flanks while the SOG agents brought up the rear. Logan had been a little worried the pilot might hold them back since he was clearly exhausted, but he moved across the broken terrain as fast as Logan did. Apparently, he wanted to get out of this place as much as the rest of them.

They'd barely gone two miles when someone ambushed them. Logan jumped on Nikolay and drove him to the ground, shoving him behind a rocky outcropping and protecting him with his body as round after round of small arms fire slammed into the ground around them.

From the disciplined, controlled way the bad guys shot at them, Logan immediately knew they weren't dealing with a ragtag collection of terrorists or Syrian military. The people shooting at them knew exactly what they were doing.

"It's a Spetsnaz team," Chasen said as he peppered the south ridgeline with slow, careful shots intended to make the bad guys duck and cover. "I don't know how, but they must have known we'd be coming this way."

"Fucking Kurds played both sides against the middle," Joe muttered. "They took our money and probably the Russian's, too, then told them know which way we went after the exchange."

"What's the plan?" Dalton shouted as he aimed the mini 40mm grenade launcher mounted on his M4 then popped a high explosive grenade toward the top of the north ridgeline.

"Get the pilot out of here alive," Joe ordered.

* * * * *

Felicia was starting to think Hayley might be a saint when the journalist showed up at her apartment door Tuesday night with pizza and a movie, asking if she needed some company.

"Being alone when you're stressed out is a bad idea," Hayley told her as she set the pizza box on the island in the kitchen.

Felicia couldn't argue with that. "I was about to call my sister and ask if she wanted to hang out. Do you mind if I invite her to join us?"

She felt horrible admitting it, but she'd been so caught up in her own crap, she hadn't even realized she hadn't talked to Stef since they had dinner together last week. She'd tried to call Stef a few times over the weekend, but had ended up having to leave messages on her voicemail.

"Of course not." Hayley smiled. "I'd love to meet her."

But, like all the other times she'd called, Stef still didn't answer.

Felicia stared pensively at the pizza box, her mind going to all kinds of places it shouldn't. She tried to tell herself she was being an alarmist, but the nagging feeling in her stomach wouldn't go away. Something was wrong with Stef. She could feel it.

"Hey," Hayley said. "You okay?"

"Yeah. I'm worried about Stef. After the kidnapping, she acted like it wasn't a big deal, but since then... I don't know, she seems...off. I've been trying to get hold of her since last week, and she's not picking up her phone." Felicia sighed. "Would you mind if I take a rain check on dinner? I want to take a run over to her dorm."

"Of course not. Want me to go with you?"

Felicia started to say no but then changed her mind. "Actually, yeah. I could use the company."

Giving Chewy a treat, Felicia stuck the pizza in the fridge then grabbed her purse. When they got to the Earl Warren dorm, Felicia led the way to Stef's room and knocked on the door. Stef's roommate, Kelly Doyle, a girl with red hair a freckles opened it.

"Is Stef here?" Felicia asked.

Kelly frowned. "She moved out a couple of months ago to live with her boyfriend off campus."

Felicia did a double take. "What?"

"Yeah. Since seniors can never get space in the dorms, Craig lives in this cool place in Downtown La Jolla. He asked Stef to live with him, and of course she said yes." Kelly folded her arms. "Heck, I'd live with them if I could. Do you know the washer and dryer in this dorm hasn't worked in a year?"

Felicia knew her sister had a pretty steady thing going with Craig, but she had no idea she'd moved in with him.

Felicia shook her head. She could care less about hogging dorm space. She had more important things to worry about. "Do you know where Craig lives?"

Kelly shook her head. "Sorry. I just know it's downtown."

"Do you know Craig's last name?" Hayley asked Felicia as they left the dorm.

"Yeah, but what good is it going to do?" Felicia said. "It's not like we can look him up in a phone book."

If those things even still existed.

When they got in Hayley's car, she pulled out her phone and dialed someone. "Without getting into a whole lot of messy details," she said to Felicia, "Kyla is a world class hacker. She'll be able to find where this guy lives."

Felicia sat there wide-eyed as Hayley chatted with the shy, quiet girl. Kyla was a hacker? How had that not come up during their conversation at lunch yesterday? And how could this girl possibly find a guy's house with nothing more than a name?

Apparently, Kyla had because fifteen minutes later, Hayley pulled up in front of a duplex in a part of town Felicia had a hard time believing any student could afford. She knew Craig was pre-med, but did he sell drugs on the side?

Craig answered Felicia's knock, smiling when he saw her. "Hey, Felicia."

"Is my sister here?" she asked sharply.

"Um, yeah. I'll go get her. Come in."

The inside of the house was as nice as the outside, and from the feminine touches around, it looked like her sister had made herself right at home.

Stef came down the steps into the foyer. Craig, thankfully, was nowhere to be seen.

"Why didn't you tell me you'd moved out of the dorms?" Felicia demanded.

The question came out harsher than she'd intended. But hell, she'd been terrified, and Stef owed her an explanation.

Stef folded her arms. "Because I figured you'd lose your mind. Apparently, I was right."

Felicia face her face heat. "I'm not mad you moved. I'm mad you didn't tell me. What if there had been an emergency?"

"You would have called me."

"I have been calling you—multiple times!" Felicia said, frustrated her sister didn't even seem to care she was upset. "You never returned my calls."

Stef at least had the dignity to look slightly ashamed. "I'm sorry. I've been really busy lately and I didn't have the energy to deal with you."

Felicia felt like someone had punched her in the stomach. "The energy to deal with me? What does that mean? When did I stop being your sister and start being a burden?"

Emotions flitted across Stef's face. Anger first then embarrassment, and finally acceptance.

"You've always been my sister, and you always will be, but you've always made it clear you see the world drastically different than I do." Stef took a deep breath. "Craig and I are engaged, Felicia. We're getting married after he graduates."

If Felicia thought she'd been floored before, it was nothing compared to what she felt now. "Married? You're not serious?"

"Yes, I am serious. Craig and I have been dating for over a year, and we've been engaged for four months."

Felicia blinked. "Why didn't you tell me?"

Stef ran her hand through her long hair. "I tried half a dozen times. But you never want to hear me, so I stopped bothering. I knew you'd freak out. Exactly like you're doing now."

"I'm freaking out because you're too young to be making decisions like this. You need to slow down and make sure you're doing the right thing. Like Mom and Dad taught us."

"No, that's what they taught you." Stef lifted her chin. "If what happened in the warehouse taught me anything it's that we don't know how long we have to spend with the people who matter. You can't waste a second of it."

"So you're going to jump into marriage with a man you barely know?" Felicia asked incredulously.

"No, I'm jumping into marriage with the man I love, and who loves me. It's about how much we love each other, not how much we've analyzed our relationship."

Felicia wanted to scream. "Planning for a life together isn't a bad thing. It's what gets you over the rough patches. If you'd thought this through, you'd see what I'm talking about. You're going to get married right before Craig goes med school? While you're still in college? How is that possibly going to work? You're never going to see each other. Hell, you won't even be able to pay the bills."

"That's not your problem, it's ours." Stef gave her an icy glare. "Maybe you should go."

Felicia silently fumed. She wasn't leaving until she'd talked some sense into her sister. She dug her cell phone out of her purse, poking the screen viciously as she pulled up Google.

"What are you doing?" Stef asked in exasperation.

"I'm showing you the statistics on divorce rates for people who marry under the age of twenty-five," Felicia said.

"I don't care," Stef said. "Stats are

your thing, not mine."

"Look at this!" Felicia said, shoving the phone in Stef's face.

Her sister slapped the phone away, making Felicia lose her grip on it. It fell with a clatter, bouncing on the wood floor. Felicia didn't even look at it. The phone was probably broken, but not as broken as her heart. Her sister had dismissed everything Felicia had tried to teach her, as if it meant nothing to her.

"Go home, Felicia," her sister said softly as she opened the door. "We're done here."

Felicia stared at her sister for a long moment, tears stinging her eyes. Blinking them back, she bent to pick up her broken phone then turned and walked out.

Chapter Eleven

LOGAN GRABBED THE back of Nikolay's flight uniform, dragging him to his feet and shoving him along the rocky path while Chasen and the other guys poured cover fire into the ridgelines along either side of them. Even with all the lead and steel coming at them, the Spetsnaz team focused on one thing—killing the pilot. As bullets spattered rocks around him and grenades exploded, Logan let instinct take over. There was only one way they were all going to survive this ambush—get out of this valley. The Russians would have to come out of hiding to chase them, and Logan liked his chances in that situation a lot more than he did sitting behind a rock waiting for a bullet to find him.

Nikolay wasn't wearing NVGs, so he couldn't see in the dark. Fortunately, he seemed to have faith in Logan and ran balls out in whichever direction Logan pointed.

For a minute there, Logan didn't think

they'd ever get out of this mess, but ten seconds later, they popped out the end of the valley and the number of rounds impacting around them dropped drastically. Somewhere off to the left, Logan heard the thud of heavy boots thumping on rocks.

Somebody—maybe a couple somebodies—were chasing him and the pilot, while the rest kept the other guys occupied.

As soon as he could, Logan steered Nikolay to the right, away from their pursuers. But the ground was rockier and started ascending. The pilot slowed down, and Logan knew this chase would be pretty short. He could feel the bad guys getting closer.

Thirty seconds later, he and Nikolay crested a low hill. The pilot gained reckless speed on the downslope, but it wouldn't help them. There'd only be another uphill climb on the other side, and by then the Russians would catch them out in the open.

Logan needed to do something besides run.

He reached out and grabbed Nikolay, dragging him to a stop and yanking him down to the ground behind a bunch of rocks not much bigger than their heads. They wouldn't stop too many bullets, but hopefully they'd provide a few seconds of concealment long enough for him to deal with the men coming behind them.

As he knelt down beside the pilot, Logan picked up a rock the size of his fist and pitched it down the slope where it hit with a clatter. Then he prayed the Russians would assume the noise had been them stumbling down the hill.

A few moments later, a figure appeared over the hill, moving way slower than Logan would have liked. Unfortunately, there wasn't anyone with him.

Shit. Logan had been sure he'd heard at least two people behind them.

He would have waited to see if a second soldier lagged behind the first, but he simply couldn't. Too much chance he and the pilot would be seen.

So he snapped his M4 to his shoulder and put three rounds through the man's chest, killing him but completely missing the other one who'd split from his buddy and circled around the hilltop to the right. By the time Logan saw him, the guy was barely fifteen feet away. They stared at each other for a split second then the Russian charged him, his weapon firing on full automatic. Knowing he was screwed, Logan charged at the Russian soldier, firing his weapon on the run.

One second they were both shooting, the next they slammed into each other like two football players on a kickoff.

The Russian soldier was big and the impact hurt like a son of a bitch. But Logan forced himself to his feet, sure he'd be dead if he didn't.

That's when he discovered three of his

bullets had hit the Russian. The Spetsnaz soldier lay dead with two holes in his stomach and one in his chest. Logan glanced down at his own body, not sure how he'd gotten through this one without buying it. Sometimes it was training; sometimes it was luck. He was still considering that when he heard a noise behind him.

He spun and saw the pilot looking around.

"Is it over?" the man asked in English not nearly as accented as Logan expected.

Logan looked at the two dead Spetsnaz soldiers on the ground, about to nod, but then he heard more gunfire behind them near the site of the original ambush. He started to check in with Chasen over his squad radio but realized he needed to get the pilot out of this area first.

He moved forward and pulled Nikolay to his feet. "We're not dead yet, but that doesn't mean it's over. We have about three miles of rough terrain to cover, so let's go."

* * * * *

"Stef didn't say where she was going?" Felicia asked the woman who resided in the other side of the duplex where her sister and Craig lived.

The woman, an elderly lady with gray hair and kind eyes, shook her head. "I'm afraid not. I was coming back from a walk this morning when I saw her and Craig get in his car with some suitcases. They left before I had a chance to ask."

Felicia sighed. She'd driven over to the duplex Stef shared with her boyfriend, fully intending to try to talk to her sister about this crazy idea of getting married before she even finished her sophomore year in college. Felicia doubted Stef would listen, but she had to try. She couldn't let her sister make such a huge mistake.

Now, she wasn't going to get the chance. Stef and Craig had already run off to get married.

Felicia would have called her sister right then, but the idiot at the cell phone store had screwed up when he'd transferred everything from her broken phone to her new one. Her work calendar was now empty, her music playlist gone, and her contact list was now a useless mess of old Yahoo email addresses and random phone numbers with no names attached. She didn't even know if she was getting texts like she was supposed to. She'd gotten a few from Heather and a couple from Hayley, but they'd come in hours after her friends had sent them. She never realized what a lifeline her phone was until then. She'd didn't have Stef's number, or even Logan's. Heck, she barely had anyone's contact info.

Fortunately, since Hayley had texted her, Felicia had her number. Thank God. Because right then, Hayley was the only person Felicia could think of who might be able to help her find Stef.

"It's me," she said when the other

woman answered. "I need a big favor."

"Anything," Hayley said.

Felicia explained the situation with Stef and her boyfriend. "Do you think Kyla might be able to do some hacking and figure out where they went?"

Hayley hesitated. "I'll see what Kyla can do, but Felicia, Stef is an adult. If she wants to run off with her boyfriend, do you think it's a good idea to run after her and try to drag her home? She isn't going to appreciate that."

Felicia's gaze went to the duplex. "I know, but I need to know where she is. I need to know she's okay."

Hayley said she'd get with Kyla and call her back as soon as she could. All Felicia could do was sigh and wonder what to do with the information if she was right about her suspicions and Stef had eloped to somewhere like Vegas.

As Felicia started her car, she realized she'd never gotten around to asking Hayley for Logan's number. She almost called her friend back, but resisted. She didn't want to be a nuisance. Besides, it wasn't like Logan would probably be getting back for a while. She'd get his number when Hayley called back later.

* * * * *

Logan glanced at his watch, shocked it was only 1100 hours. Shit. The pilot's debriefing had only been going for an hour. God, it felt like it had been days. Probably because it was so damn boring. Logan knew the stuff Nikolay was telling the CIA and Navy analysts about the new Russian aircraft was very valuable, but it was dull as hell. Thank God SEALs rescued people for a living and didn't do intel analysis. He'd be bored out of his mind.

On the upside, the Russian pilot had demanded Logan and the rest of his Team accompany him back to the States. For some reason, he felt safer with SEAL Team 5 than the CIA. That meant they got to come home much earlier than he expected.

Logan leaned over to tell Chasen he was going to grab some coffee then slipped out of the conference room. While he could use the caffeine, it was really an excuse to go downstairs to the little boxes where they had to store their cell phones.

He sent a quick text to Felicia, letting her know he was back and asking if she wanted to get together that night. He hung around for as long as he could get away with, but she didn't text back. Disappointed, he tossed his phone back in the box and went back to the conference room, stopping to grab coffee for him and Chasen on the way.

Four long hours later, the CIA called it a night and Logan was finally free to get the hell out of there. He'd thought for sure Felicia would have texted him back by now, but he didn't have any messages from her.

The smart thing to do would probably be to call her, but instead he drove over to her condo. Considering it was a Saturday night, there was a very real possibility she might be out with another guy. That thought sucked.

But when he knocked on her door, Felicia opened it right away.

"You're back!" she said.

Before he could say anything, she kissed him hard then wrapped her arms around him and hugged him fiercely. A second later, she took his hand and tugged him inside.

"When did you get home?" she asked.

"This morning," he said.

She looked so beautiful standing there in a pair of shorts and a tank top, her hair loose around her shoulders. All he wanted to do was pull her into his arms and kiss her until they were both gasping for air. But if he did, they'd end up in bed, and he had something important he needed to say to her first.

He ran his hand through his hair. "Can we talk?"

Felicia stiffened at his words, her face suddenly pale. Okay, maybe that hadn't been the best way to start the conversation.

She motioned him toward the couch. "Yeah, of course. What do you want to talk about?"

He sat and rested his forearms on his thighs. "About us—you and me."

Logan cursed himself. Of course *us* meant her and him. Who the hell else could it mean, the guys on his SEAL Team?

"What I'm trying to say is that I think you're great," he said. "Better than great even."

Oh hell, this was getting worse! Why the hell couldn't he figure out what to say? It shouldn't be this hard. *Just tell her you really like her, you dumbass moron!*

Putting his thoughts into words was a lot harder to do than he'd ever imagined. How could he tell her how he felt, when he didn't know for sure himself?

"You know the feeling you get when you find the absolutely perfect pair of boots," he said. "Boots you could walk a hundred miles in and never get a blister? Or when you wrap your hands around the grip of a new pistol and instinctively feel like it was made for you? Do you know what I'm saying?"

Felicia stared at him. "No, I don't have a clue what you're saying. I'm not even sure if you're speaking English."

The hell with trying to finesse his way through this. "Felicia, I think we have something special between us, and I want to keep seeing you."

Logan exhaled so hard it felt like he might pass out. But it was over with. The bandage had been ripped off. All his hopes and fears were lying out there clear as day.

Or not.

Felicia stared at him in confusion for a moment, but then, suddenly, realization dawned on her face. "Are you trying to say you're in love with me?"

Okay, that was rather blunt and totally unexpected. It also forced him to examine exactly how he thought about Felicia, which he'd been trying to avoid getting too deep into regardless of the advice Chasen had given him in Syria.

Was he in love with Felicia? Maybe, But he was worried to even admit it, especially since he didn't know if she felt the same way. He might not be a coward when it came to getting shot at, but having his heart torn out by a woman he cared for wasn't something he was thrilled about.

But she'd asked the question, and if he took a step back from the truth now, he'd never get the chance to go there with her again. He wasn't willing to turn his back on a shot at something amazing with Felicia, even if it was a really long shot in seriously high winds.

"I know this should be a simple question, Felicia, but the truth is, I've never been in love before. I don't think I've even come close," he told her. "I guess I assumed getting serious with a woman would have to wait until after I retired from the Navy. But sometimes things happen when we're not looking—like meeting you."

He took a deep breath then sighed and started again. "Look, I hate slapping labels on things as difficult to get my hands around as how I feel about you. All I know is that when I'm with you, I feel like there's something in the world that matters beyond being a SEAL and doing the job. I know it's crazy since we've barely known each other for more than a couple of weeks, but it's true."

Logan studied Felicia's face, hoping to get a read on her. But she gave him nothing. She merely gazed back at him blankly. Like she was too shocked by his confession to even react.

Having no choice at this point, he decided to keep going. He was a man, dammit. If he was going to dig his own grave, he'd sure as hell make sure it was deep enough.

"If being really happy when I'm with you and worrying like crazy about you when I'm not means I'm in love with you," he said. "Then, yeah, I guess I am."

Chapter Twelve

FELICIA BLINKED. LOGAN loved her. Well, he hadn't said it in so many words, and certainly not in the way you typically saw in the movies. But, still, he had said the word *love*. Of all the things she'd expected Logan to say when he'd showed up at the door, love definitely hadn't been one of them.

When she'd opened the door, she been so happy to see him standing there safe and sound she'd wanted to cry—or laugh. She didn't know which.

Then he'd said he wanted to "talk." Those words, along with the serious expression on his face had her freaking out on the inside. She'd thought for sure he'd been going to tell her it wasn't working out between them. That his time away had given him a new perspective, and he didn't want to see her again.

Instead he'd gone into a rambling soliloquy involving boots and blisters and pistol grips. She'd been so lost, she'd felt like pulling out her new cell phone to ask Siri if she had a clue what the hell Logan was talking about.

But he'd floored her by saying he thought there was something between them and he wanted to keep seeing her. Just like that, his bumbling, stumbling words made a strange kind of sense. Logan liked her—as in seriously liked her.

Felicia didn't know why she'd asked him if he loved her. Maybe it was the stuff Stef had thrown in her face about what you feel for a man being far more important than how long you've know him. Or maybe there was simply a part of her that was falling in love with Logan, too.

A few days ago, she'd practically laughed in her sister's face when Stef tried to convince her love was the only thing that mattered. Now Logan said he loved her and that there was something special between them.

The craziest thing of all was that everything Logan said made complete and total sense. She felt the exact same way about him.

She did a double take.

It was true. She was in love—or at least falling in love—with a man she'd known all of two weeks. It should have scared the hell out of her, but instead it made her feel happier than she'd ever been.

It suddenly occurred to her that Logan

was still talking and she hadn't heard a word he'd said. She tuned in to hear him apologizing for springing all this on her so suddenly and for coming over here in the first place.

"My gut told me this wouldn't work, that I was pushing you too fast, but I took a chance. I'm sorry."

Before Felicia could say anything, Logan got to his feet and headed for the door. He must have taken her stunned silence to mean she didn't feel the same way about him as he did about her. That couldn't be further from the truth.

She jumped up and grabbed his arm. When he turned, she wrapped her arms around his neck, dragging him down for a kiss.

Logan immediately kissed her back, his hands grabbing her ass and pull her tightly against him.

Throwing caution to the wind and going with her instincts might be insane, but she knew in her heart it was right.

Just when it seemed the heat of their mouths on one another might lead to something combustible right there in the entryway of her apartment, Logan broke the kiss and looked down at her.

"I'm guessing this means you still want to keep seeing me?" he asked.

She thumped him on the shoulder, which probably hurt her hand far more than it hurt his shoulder. "Of course I want to keep seeing you! Are you crazy?"

His mouth twitched. "I think that goes with saying. It's the only thing that explains how I could be falling in love with a woman I've known for two weeks and have slept with only once."

Felicia smiled. "Well, I am really good in bed."

He chuckled. "Well, there you go. That explains everything."

She laughed with him, feeling a weight being lifted from her shoulders she'd never known was there. But she was the first one to turn serious as she realized there were a few things she needed to say to him.

"You might have surprised me a little by saying what you did, but it doesn't mean I wasn't happy to hear it. I spent the whole time you were away thinking about us, what we had, and where we were going. I'll admit, I've always been the kind to take things slowly. I've always assumed I would meet this great guy, and we would spend years getting to know each other, planning out each and every step of our relationship."

"But?" he prompted.

"But then I met you and the whole carefully laid out plan I had for my life flipped upside down."

"Is that so bad?" he asked.

She gazed up into his beautiful eyes. "If you'd asked me a few days ago, the answer would have been yes. But right now the answer is definitely not. In fact, I get the feeling someday, I'm going to look back on this moment and realize it's the best thing that ever happened to me."

Logan smiled, then his mouth came down on hers again and she felt her body melt into his. With a groan, he slipped one arm behind her knees and scooped her up then headed for her bedroom.

Once there, they undressed each other slowly, hands roaming everywhere. When they were both naked, Felicia climbed into bed and spread her legs wide. Logan joined her, settling comfortably between them.

There wasn't any teasing this time. Instead, Logan slipped inside, taking her breath away. His mouth came down to nuzzle her neck, tracing kisses everywhere as he began to thrust in steady rhythm. She wrapped her arms and legs around him, pulling him deeper.

Felicia had no idea how long they moved like that together, but at some point Logan's thrusts got faster, making her moan every time he bottomed out inside her.

"Harder," she whispered in his ear, knowing she was close and wanting him to come with her.

Logan obeyed, lifting his head to look down at her as he pounded into her.

They came together as they gazed into each other's eyes. She'd never done anything quite like it before, and it was the most powerful thing she'd ever felt. Making love to a man she loved probably had a lot to do with how hard she orgasmed, too. Either way, she wouldn't complain.

Felicia lay on his chest afterward, listening to the steady beat of his heart beneath her ear. She smiled. If this was what it meant to be with the man she loved, she could definitely get used to it.

She was on the verge of drifting off to sleep when Logan gently nudged her awake. "I was so busy worrying about whether you were going to slam the door in my face when I got here, I didn't ask if everything is ready for the sunrise wedding tomorrow?"

Crap. She was glad he'd said something. She'd completely forgotten she needed to get up early tomorrow. As she sat up to set the alarm clock, she filled Logan in on the last second changes the bride had requested.

"How are things with Stef?" he asked when she cuddled up against him again.

"Not great," Felicia admitted, explaining about the argument with her sister. "According to Hayley's friend Kyla, Stef and her boyfriend are at a hotel in Vegas. They've been there since Thursday."

"Do you think they're getting married?"

She nodded against his shoulder. "They probably already are. And before you say it, I know she's a grown woman who doesn't need an older sister making decisions for her. But it doesn't mean I'm not worried about her or concerned she's running off to get married for all the wrong reasons."

Logan ran his fingers up and down her arm. "I get that. But have you ever thought maybe your sister has stumbled across the person she's meant to be with?"

Felicia smiled. "If someone had said that to me a couple of hours ago, I would have laughed and insisted following your heart is the worst way to start any relationship. But now, considering I admitted to being in love with a guy I met only a couple of weeks ago, I suppose I have to agree Stef is on to something."

"What are you going to do?" he asked softly. "When Stef gets back, I mean."

She shrugged. "I'm not sure, but whatever it is, it will probably start with an apology. Though I'm guessing my sister is never going to let me live down the fact I fell in love with you so fast. She'll probably take great pleasure in pointing out I have cheese slices in my fridge that have been together longer than we have."

Logan chuckled.

Chapter Thirteen

LOGAN GROANED AS his phone rang. He ignored it, sure it was Felicia's and not his. Then he remembered she'd gotten up and left a while ago so she could get to the beach and pull off the sunrise wedding. He said he'd go with her, but she'd told him to stay in bed and sleep in. He'd felt badly about falling back asleep while she went to work, but he was too exhausted to argue. She'd be home before noon then they could spend the rest of the day together.

He was thinking of the sexy kiss she'd given him before leaving when the damn phone rang again.

Cursing under his breath, he threw back the blankets and rolled out of bed, ignoring the perturbed look Chewy gave him from the bottom of the bed as he dug through the piles of clothes on the floor until he found his phone. Seeing all those casually discarded clothes reminded him of the sex they'd had the night before, which only made him think of what they could do later today. The thought started his cock hardening.

He looked down at his phone, relieved to see it wasn't HQ with another mission. He didn't recognize the number though. He thumbed the green button.

"Logan, it's Heather. Is Felicia still there?"

Logan glanced at the clock on the nightstand to see it was after 0600 already. "No. Felicia left an hour ago."

"Are you sure?" Heather asked. "She never got to the wedding location, and the bride and groom are getting nervous. I've called and left her a dozen messages, but she hasn't called me back."

"Hold on a minute," he said as he padded out into the hall and downstairs to the living room. Surely, he would have heard Felicia moving around if she were still home. As he'd thought, she wasn't there. Her purse was gone, too.

"She's not here," he told Heather. "Maybe she got caught in traffic."

"On a Sunday morning?"

Yeah, that didn't make a whole hell of a lot of sense. His gut told him something wasn't right.

Logan walked over to look out the front window. Felicia's car was still parked out in her space.

Shit.

"Heather, I'll call you later. You're

going to have to handle the wedding on your own."

She said something, but Logan hung up. Running upstairs, he pulled on his clothes then hurried outside. He headed straight for her car in the early morning light, hoping the hood would be warm or there'd be a message sitting under the windshield. Nothing. Just a cold car with a little morning condensation covering the windows.

Now he had a really bad feeling.

He pulled out his phone and hit the speed dial for Felicia. She picked up on the first ring.

"Felicia, are you okay?" Relief rushed through him. "Heather has been calling you for the last hour. Where are you?"

"Felicia can't come to the phone right now," a man's thickly accented Russian voice said. "She's a little tied up at the moment."

Logan's hand tightened on the phone. Even though he'd never heard the man's voice before, he instinctively knew it was Illarion Volkov.

"What do you want Volkov?"

"I want to kill the police officers who arrested my men. I want to punish your woman for refusing to do as I told her. Most of all, I want to make you pay for killing my brother. So, as you can see, Petty Officer Dunn, there are a great many things I want. But for now, I will forego my wants in return for one thing."

"What's that?" Logan asked, though he

was pretty sure he already knew.

"A traitorous Russian pilot named Nikolay Maksimov. Bring him to me, and I will give you back your woman safe and unmarred—for the most part anyway."

Logan tensed at the threat, but he kept his cool. Volkov was taunting him. "What makes you think I'll be able to get anywhere near the Russian pilot? The CIA are watching him like a hawk."

"I'm sure a man as clever as you will come up with a way. If not, I'll be forced to take out my frustrations on pretty little Felicia."

Logan swallowed hard. "How do I know you haven't hurt her already?"

"You don't," Volkov said. "So I suggest you hurry up and bring me the pilot."

"What do you hope to get out of this, Volkov? You can't seriously think you'll be able to sneak him across the border into Mexico. You got away with that the first time a couple of weeks ago, but it won't work again. The CIA will have everything shut down the moment they realize Maksimov is missing."

"You let me worry about that. You worry about what's going to happen to your woman if you don't get here in time. You really don't want to see what I do when I get angry."

Whether he knew it or not, Volkov had admitted he planned on killing the pilot. Not shocking.

"Let's say I'm able to get my hands on the pilot," Logan told him. "Where do I bring him?"

"Same warehouse as the first time," Volkov said. "But before you think you can assault the place like I heard you did when you killed my brother, you can forget it. You have no way of knowing if I'll be inside waiting with a gun to your woman's head or watching from three blocks away with my fingers on the trigger of a bomb waiting to blow Felicia to small pink pieces. Either way, if you show up with anyone other than my pilot, your pretty little girlfriend will die."

Logan ground his jaw. "I'll be there with the pilot and no one else in an hour, but if you've hurt Felicia, I'll kill you the same way I killed your brother."

He hung up before Volkov had a chance to reply and headed for his SUV at a run, hitting the speed dial button for Chasen as he ran.

"I've got trouble," he said the moment his friend answered. "That Russian bastard Volkov is back and he grabbed Felicia. I need you to get some of the other guys and do a long distance reconnaissance of the same warehouse we hit the last time. But be careful. It's possible he's set up in another building watching the target warehouse. There might also be a bomb involved."

"Where are you going to be?" Chasen asked.

Logan appreciated his friend's complete

and unquestioning loyalty. Of all the things that made the SEALs so amazing, this was more important than their toughness, their weapons, or their training. Their total commitment to each other made the Teams function. And he needed that loyalty right now to save Felicia's life...again.

"I'll be there in less than an hour," Logan told him. "But first I have to stop by and pick up some bait without letting the CIA know I'm taking it."

"You're bringing Nikolay?" Chasen asked, clearly surprised. "How do you plan to get him to come with you?"

"I'm simply going to remind him I saved his ass and ask for his help."

"And if it doesn't work?"

"Then I'm going to knock him over the head and carry him out over my shoulder."

"Need any backup?" Chasen asked. "I can't imagine Joe and his SOG guys are going to stand around watching while you drag off their newest intel asset."

Understatement there. "No, I'm good. Get to the warehouse and figure out where Volkov has Felicia. Call me as soon as you know what's going on. If Volkov is in the warehouse with Felicia, my plan is to go in and keep him distracted until you come in with the cavalry."

"Simple plan. I like it." Chasen said. "I'll have info for you in forty minutes.

Logan hung up and sped out of the parking lot, thinking about how he'd get the

Russian pilot away from the CIA. They had him in one of the temporary officer quarters on the base. Physically getting into the place would be easy, but getting in without alarming the CIA agents or the SOG guys watching the place would be a bit more complicated.

* * * * *

Felicia sat tied to the same chair her sister had been trussed up in only two weeks earlier. How the heck could this be happening to her all over again? Wasn't there some law of probability that said if you got kidnapped by a psychotic Russian killer once, it was statistically impossible for it to ever happen again?

Except it had happened again. Illarion Volkov had slipped up behind her and gotten a hand around her mouth as she got in her car this morning. She'd fought him, but the Russian had wrapped his other arm around her waist, picked her up, and dragged her to his van.

There'd been another guy driving the vehicle, but shortly after dropping her and Volkov off at the warehouse, the man had left on foot. Now she was alone with the former Russian Special Forces soldier. The man sat in a matching chair only a few feet away, regarding her like a bug he wanted to smash.

But as scared as she was for herself, she was even more terrified for Logan. She'd heard Volkov talking to him on the phone and seen the look of hatred on the Russian's face as he spoke. The son of a bitch wanted Logan dead and he wanted to be the one to kill him.

She prayed Logan wouldn't come, but at the same time, she knew he would.

"Logan didn't want to kill your brother," she said. "But your brother tried to kill my sister. Logan didn't have a choice."

Volkov glared at her. "Do you think I care why he killed Peter? He spilled my family's blood. Your Navy SEAL will die right after he watches me kill you. If he brings the pilot and his SEAL friends, all the better. I can kill them, too. If not, I will be satisfied with the two of you."

Felicia shuddered. Volkov was insane. She could see it in his eyes. "You don't even care if you live through this, do you?"

Volkov stood and walked over to her. She cringed, afraid he might kill her right then, but instead he grabbed a handful of her hair and jerked her head back. She fought and struggled against the duct tape holding her arms down to the chair, ignoring the way her skin chafed. But the tape holding her down didn't give, and there wasn't anything she could do as he yanked her head back so hard she thought for sure he would break her neck. She screamed in pain, but the sound was muffled as he stuffed a rag into her mouth then tied it in place with another length of cloth.

He glanced at his watch. "Your boyfriend will be here soon. I'm sure he'll try something heroic in a sad attempt to save your life, so I'm going to leave you here on your own. But don't worry. I'll be back in time to see his face when he realizes he can't save you. It will make all of this worthwhile."

She tried to tell him he was crazy, but nothing got through the gag except muffled grunts. He ignored her anyway, turning and walking out of the office with a laugh. A moment later, she heard a metal door slam.

Felicia struggled against the tape again, but it wouldn't budge. She briefly considered pushing the chair over, thinking maybe she could get it to break, but then she imagined the back of her head slamming into the concrete floor and decided against it. Besides, the metal chair didn't look like it would break if you hit it with a sledgehammer.

She forced herself to calm down and try to think of a way out of this situation, but ultimately the only way she would get out of this alive was if Logan rescued her. He was probably on his way there right now. He might be bringing the pilot and some of his friends, or he might be coming alone.

She tried to tell herself rescuing hostages and dealing with very bad people like Volkov was what SEALs did every day. That didn't mean she wasn't freaking out. The thought of Logan getting hurt her made her lightheaded.

That's when Felicia she realized how far she'd fallen for Logan. They'd talked a lot last night about being in love and wanting to have something long term, but those had been words. She hadn't understood what it meant to totally love a man until this moment as she realized she didn't even care what happened to her as long as he was okay.

Oh God. Just be okay...please.

* * * * *

"Nikolay got a message to me through headquarters," Logan told the SOG agent sitting in a car outside the temporary officer quarters. "He wants to talk to me about something."

The SOG guy regarded him thoughtfully. "No one told me anything about it."

Logan shrugged. "I just found out about it when my boss called and told me to get the hell over here and be nice to this guy—whatever the hell that means. I'd much rather be sleeping in on a Sunday, but nobody bothered to ask for my opinion."

The guy laughed. "I hear you. At our level, we're basically mushrooms. The people in charge leave us in the dark and feed us shit."

"I'll be in and out of there as fast as I can," Logan promised.

He walked up to the small duplex unit that served as one of the temporary housing billets for senior officers who visited the base. Due to the sensitive nature of the pilot's identity, headquarters had put the man in the most remote building they had. That made it easy for the CIA to keep an eye on their asset while at the same time not treating the valuable intelligence resource like a prisoner.

Logan tapped on the door then let himself into the small apartment. Like every military style billeting room he'd ever been in, the place was filled with generic furniture and painted in boring colors.

Nikolay sat on the couch, reading a magazine, and he looked up in surprise. "Logan, what are you doing here?"

Logan considered coming up with a bullshit reason to get the Russian pilot out of the house but quickly dismissed the idea. It would likely cause more problems than it would help in the long run, especially when the man figured out what was going on.

"I need your help," Logan said. "The Russian government has sent a former Spetsnaz soldier named Volkov to get you back, maybe even kill you. He's kidnapped my girlfriend and he wants to exchange her for you."

Nikolay's eyes widened. "The man is here on the base?"

Logan shook his head. "No. He has her in a warehouse near here. I have a plan to get her out, but I need you to be the bait."

Nikolay stared at him, and for a second, Logan thought maybe the guy didn't understand what he'd said, but then the pilot nodded. "You have not told the CIA people about this, have you?"

Logan shook his head. "No. They're good people, especially the ones with us over in Syria, but I don't trust them the way I trust the men on my SEAL Team."

Nikolay nodded. "I will help you."

Damn. Logan had expected some kind of resistance. "You know I'll do anything I can to keep you safe, but I need you to understand, I'm not even sure I can get my Team and I out of this safely. Volkov is dangerous. I'm doing this to save my girlfriend's life, no matter the cost."

Nikolay smiled slowly. "I understand. I know what it's like to have a woman worth risking everything for. I will help, no matter the cost. It's what I owe you for risking your life to save mine."

Logan imagined there was a hell of a story somewhere behind those few sentences, and hopefully, someday, he'd get a chance to ask Nikolay about it. But now wasn't the time.

Nikolay tossed the magazine side and headed for the front door, but Logan stopped him. "Not that way. There's a guard out there we need to avoid. You'll have to go out a window along the back of the building. Go in a wide circle around the duplex, and I'll pick you up on the main street outside."

"And from there?"

"I have some of my teammates already moving in on the warehouse, pinpointing where Volkov is," Logan said. "Once we know, we go in together to distract him then do whatever's necessary to get Felicia away from him."

Nikolay was halfway out the window

when he stopped to look back at Logan. "If we make it through this, you are likely to get into much trouble, right?"

"Probably," Logan agreed. "But if we get through this, it's a cost I'll gladly pay."

"This Felicia is worth much to you, yes?"

"She's worth everything to me," he said, meaning it from the bottom of his heart.

* * * * *

It felt like Felicia had been tied to the chair for hours before the outer door opened again. She tensed, fearing Volkov was coming back. She almost fainted when she saw Logan, both because she was relieved to see him and terrified at the same time. There was a shorter dark-haired man with him. He must be the Russian pilot Volkov had mentioned.

She shook her head, making as much noise as she could through the gag in an effort to get Logan's attention and trying to tell him he was in danger. Logan ran to her side and yanked the gag out of her mouth.

"It's a trap," she told him urgently. "Volkov is planning to kill us all."

But rather than run, Logan and the pilot began to work at the tape holding her to the chair, ripping it away slowly to avoid hurting her. "Logan, stop! You don't understand. He's coming!"

"Your man understands," Volkov said from out in the warehouse. "He doesn't care. He knows this is only going to end when one of us is dead."

Heart in her throat, Felicia watched as Logan stood up and spun around, a small weapon coming out from behind his back so fast she could barely follow it. He stood facing the doorway of the little office they were in, moving the pistol back and forth as he waited for Volkov to come into view. While he did, the pilot kept tearing at the tape on her right arm, ignoring what went on behind him.

"I'm surprised you brought the pilot with you," Volkov said, his voice closer now. "The Russian government would have preferred I brought him back alive to face his punishment for desertion, but they'll be happy if he's dead, too."

"It doesn't have to go down like this." Logan said in a loud voice. "You know I have other people closing in on the warehouse right now. You're not going to make it out of this."

"He's insane," Felicia told Logan as the pilot got one of her arms free and began to work on the other. "I don't think he cares about living through this."

"She is right," Volkov agreed. "I don't care. But then again, I've rarely cared. It's what helps me survive impossible situations."

Logan looked like he might say something, but he didn't get a chance because Volkov suddenly came into view outside the office and started firing into the room with an automatic weapon of some kind.

Logan threw himself in her direction,

taking both her and the pilot to the floor with him. The last of the tape holding her left arm down tore loose, freeing her from the chair and allowing her and the pilot to crawl across the floor to hide behind the desk. It didn't offer much protection, but it was better than being out in the open.

The sounds of glass breaking and bullets hitting concrete reverberated around the small space until Felicia thought she might go deaf. But she kept moving for the relative safety offered by the metal desk as the pilot tried to keep himself between her and the incoming bullets.

She expected Logan to join them, but instead he stood up and sprinted toward the row of broken windows, launching himself through them.

Felicia screamed his name and tried to get up, but the pilot grabbed her and pulled her back down. She fought him, but he wouldn't let go, and she could only listen as the gunfire got even faster and louder. There was no way a person could live through so many bullets being fired in his direction. Logan would get himself killed!

After what seemed like forever, the shooting finally stopped. She elbowed the pilot in the ribs hard enough to make him grunt in pain then ran for the door of the office. She couldn't stop the tears of relief flooding her eyes when she saw Logan standing there looking down at the unmoving body of the Russian mercenary.

Hurrying over to him, Felicia wrapped Logan in a fierce embrace even as she realized they weren't alone. Chasen, Dalton, Nash, and Kurt were standing there watching them, pistols held casually down at their sides.

"I was so worried about you," Logan said, his voice hoarse in her ear as he squeezed her tightly.

She pulled away to stared at him. "Worried about me? You were the idiot running toward the guy with the gun. What the heck did you think you were doing?"

He must have done something with his weapon because he brought both hands up to cup her face. "I was doing whatever I had to keep you safe."

"Well, thank you, but don't ever scare me like that again," she told him. "I thought I was going to lose you."

He smiled. "That's never going to happen. I promise. I'll always be there to keep you safe and love you."

Her heart melted. Going up on tiptoe, she kissed him, totally forgetting about the other people around them

"That's all very romantic and stuff," Dalton drawled. "But I don't suppose you two know where our pilot is?"

Felicia pulled back with a laugh. "He's behind the desk in the office. I thumped him in the ribs. I guess I hit him a little harder than I thought."

Dalton walked into the office, stepping

around the worst of the glass until he could see behind the desk. "Somebody call for an ambulance. Nash, get in here and start doing some of that medic shit you do. Nikolay has been hit."

Felicia and Logan followed Nash into the office. The Russian pilot was lying flat on his back, his hands pressed to a bleeding wound in his stomach. That's why he'd grunted so loudly when she'd elbowed him. She'd hit him right where he'd been shot. And he had gotten the wound protecting her.

She watched nervously as Nash ripped away Nikolay's shirt and began tending the wound.

Nikolay smiled at her. "Don't worry. I will be okay."

"Nash?" Logan asked.

His friend nodded. "He's going to need surgery for sure, but he'll make it."

"They're on the way," Kurt said from the doorway. "Along with half the federal and state law enforcement. This place is about to get very crowded."

They were still hovering around Nikolay when the ambulance and cops showed up. That's when the questions began. But at least she was better at answering them this time.

* * * * *

Felicia was exhausted by the time Logan brought her home. The questioning from the CIA and the Navy had been much worse this time, and Logan was probably looking forward to days of additional interrogations so the CIA could fume about him getting their Russian intel asset damaged. Luckily, Nikolay would be okay, if perhaps off his feet for a while. He'd already come out of surgery at the hospital and, according to Nash, who'd ridden in the ambulance with the pilot, everything had gone well.

While Logan made her a sandwich, she called Heather and found out the sunrise wedding had gone off without a hitch. Heather had been worried sick about her and when Felicia admitted she'd gotten kidnapped again, her friend threatened to run right over and check on her. But Felicia assured Heather she was fine and Logan was taking good care of her.

She hung up and watched Logan finish making the sandwich. It was hard to believe a man who could handle a weapon like him— fight like him—could also be so gentle. How the hell had she stumbled across such a perfect man?

Suddenly Felicia realized that while she'd talked about being in love with him, she'd never said the words out loud.

Sliding off the stool, she walked around the island. He stopped what he was doing to look at her.

"I love you. More than I could ever have imagined," she said. "I love you so much I'm starting to understand why Stef ran off to Vegas to get married. That's how much I want to be with you right now."

Logan grinned and kissed her. "I love you too, just as much. But we don't need to get married in the next three days to know that." He caressed her cheek. "So, let's not run off to Vegas, okay? We can take our time and have the perfect wedding you've been planning for everyone else. Whenever you're ready."

She knew it wasn't a real proposal and that when Logan did ask her, it would be a major moment. But as far as she was concerned, he'd asked her to marry him and she'd already said yes. Everything else would be a formality.

What the heck kind of wedding planner was she?

"I'm okay with that." She smiled. "As long as it isn't a sunrise wedding."

Logan chuckled. "Why not? I think you'd look beautiful with the first rays of sunlight hitting your face as we say our vows."

"Maybe," she agreed with a laugh. "But I'd rather be awake for my vows if you don't mind?"

"Not at all," he said. "You ready to eat?"

She looked down at the sandwich then back at him. "I've decided there's something else I'd rather do first. If it's okay with you?"

He smiled as if reading her mind. "That will always be okay with me."

Taking her hand, he led her out of the kitchen and upstairs.

Chapter Fourteen

LOGAN WALKED INTO Felicia's office to see her and Heather leaning over a table with Stef, their noses buried deep in a bunch of books full of colored fabric swatches, invitations, pictures of flowers and wedding gowns.

Felicia and her sister had worked out their differences a few days after Stef and her boyfriend had gotten back and they were now planning Stef's wedding, one bigger and more colorful than the first small event in Vegas.

"Hey!" Felicia came over to kiss him. "You're just in time to help pick out the color of the groom's cummerbunds."

"Shouldn't the groom be in charge of that?" Logan asked.

"Yeah, but he's too busy with finals to help out," Stef said. "He agreed to go with whatever we selected."

Huh. That could be dangerous.

From the way Felicia regarded him

from the corner of her eye, Logan suspected this was some kind of test. She hadn't said much about their own wedding lately, but he knew she thought about it.

"What color are you wearing, Stef?" he asked. "Isn't the groom's cummerbund supposed to match your gown or the colors of your bouquet?"

He'd vaguely remembered overhearing Melissa talking about it to some of the other women at a cookout once. It must have been the right thing to say because Felicia's mouth curved into a smile.

After they'd settled that, Stef pulled up her invite list on her laptop. "Everyone from the Team is coming right, plus their girlfriends, wives, significant others, etc.?"

"Yup," he said.

Although he wasn't so sure about one or two of the girlfriends. The guys would bring someone, but maybe not the girls they were with right now. Especially Dalton. The guy changed women like other men changed their underwear.

"How about Nikolay?" Felicia asked. "Will he be able to come?"

Logan shook his head. The Russian pilot had already recovered from his wound, but he wouldn't be going to any weddings, at least not for a while.

"Afraid not. The CIA has already put him into their protection program. He's probably living in Idaho somewhere by now."

Felicia and Stef looked bummed.

They'd both stopped in to see the man several times while he recovered from his injuries, and they'd become good friends.

"Is your boss still pissed at you?" Stef asked.

Logan snorted. "That's an understatement."

He'd been getting reamed out nearly every day for the past month by Commander Hunt. The man was furious Logan had not only gone up against a psycho Russian mercenary—twice—but he'd drawn the other SEALs into it as well. The incident had made both the local papers and the national news, and attention like this wasn't the kind of attention the SEALs liked.

There was also the issue of stealing the CIA's intel asset away from them and getting him shot. That hadn't gone over well at headquarters. Logan had barely avoided getting court marshaled.

"You have enough time to get lunch?" Felicia asked when they wandered over to the other side of the room to have some privacy.

"I wish," he said. "I have to get back to the shop. Unfortunately, I'll probably have to work late tonight. I wanted to see you for a little while we're both still awake."

Felicia wrapped her arms around him. "I'll take any time with you I can get."

She leaned forward and kissed him, surreptitiously slipping her hand down to caress the front of his uniform pants. He hardened immediately at her touch. "If I'm asleep by the time you get home, wake me up."

"Mmm," he breathed.

On the other side of the room, Stef groaned. "You know we can hear you guys, right? You're supposed to be the more mature sister in this family."

Logan and Felicia laughed.

"Love you," she said before he left to head back to work.

"Love you, too," he told her.

Man, he was never going to get tired of saying that.

* * * * *

Want more hunky SEALs?
Then check out Chasen Ward's story:
SEAL FOR HER PROTECTION, Book 1 in
my *SEALs OF CORONADO* Series.

Also look for TEXAS SEAL, releasing
November 2016.

ABOUT PAIGE

Paige Tyler is a *New York Times* and *USA Today* Bestselling Author of sexy, romantic suspense and paranormal romance. She and her very own military hero (also known as her husband) live on the beautiful Florida coast with their adorable fur baby (also known as their dog). Paige graduated with a degree in education, but decided to pursue her passion and write books about hunky alpha males and the kick-butt heroines who fall in love with them.

She is represented by Bob Mecoy.

www.paigetylertheauthor.com

35464858R00099